ARROW
OF DESIRE

Elizabeth McBride

AVALON BOOKS
NEW YORK

PRINTED IN THE UNITED STATES OF AMERICA
ON ACID-FREE PAPER
BY HADDON CRAFTSMEN, BLOOMSBURG, PENNSYLVANIA

To J.F. and M.G., who showed me Scotland.

Bring me my bow of burning gold,
Bring me my arrow of desire.

—WILLIAM BLAKE

Preface

In the far north of the island of Britain, there once lived a people called the Picts. We know only a few things about them. They created huge standing stones, heavily engraved with elaborate designs. They chose their kings from a line of royal women rather than men. And their warriors were so fierce that the Romans could not conquer them.

The Picts had many enemies. Chief among them were the Britons, who lived to the south and fought with the Picts generation after generation. There were also the Scots—invaders from Ireland who had settled on the western coast of Britain hundreds of years earlier and named their territory Dal Riata. Then, one day, a new enemy arrived in dragonships: the Danes. With a horrible savagery, the Danes burned fields, raped women, and enslaved children. And prompted events that changed the course of history.

Chapter One

The Irish Coast, 795 A.D.

Is this what death is like? Gormach mac Nechtan wondered to himself. He peered into the vapor, thick as guilt, that was creeping toward him up the beach. The air was so cold it threatened to still his heart.

There was no sign of the man he was waiting for. But then, the Irish mist revealed nothing until it chose.

Gormach shifted restlessly on the boulder. Waiting was difficult. It gave him too much time to think.

What would the legacy of this day be? In years to come, when he was deep in his grave and the harpers sang of his deeds, would he be blessed or would he be cursed for what he was about to do?

The sea whispered at his feet, but he could not understand its answer.

Ah! Footsteps. Gormach's sharp warrior's ears heard the soft scraping in the sand. One man. *Good.* The Irish king was keeping his side of the bargain.

He had agreed to meet the Irish king alone and was well aware that he was risking his life to do so. But if he had brought his men with him, no matter how peaceful the cause, blood would have been spilled. Hatred between the Picts and the Irish was as ancient as fire, and as consuming.

1

Gormach stood, and slipped his sword from its sheath. Best to be ready for trickery.

He listened hard for any sound that might come from the hulking cliff on his right—the pad of a stealthy foot, a treacherous breath—but he heard nothing there.

The sea throbbed steadily on his left. The crunch of oncoming footsteps grew louder.

Inexplicably, Gormach thought of his wife, she who had died long ago. Her image rose from a secret spot in his heart: her tall and slender body, her fair hair, the intelligent face that he admired more than he had ever let her know. What would have been her opinion of this? She was the royal one. Would she have resisted longer? Fought harder? Gormach didn't think so. His wife had been practical, even in her youth.

And then the man appeared out of the mist, like a ghost from the Otherworld, with a brown woolen cloak pulled up over his head. He stopped two paces from Gormach.

I could kill him with one thrust, Gormach mused, staring into the man's pale eyes.

They stood in silence until the Irishman spoke. "I am Colman mac Morgand, King of Ardara in the province of Ulster." His voice was low and measured and thickly accented.

Gormach nodded once. No need to introduce himself. Lone Picts did not appear on the north coast of Ireland very often.

The Irishman squinted. His blue eyes were as sharp as flintstone. "Your son will marry my daughter?"

Gormach nodded again.

"Do you wish to see her?"

Gormach thought on that a moment. He was curious. But he cast the impulse aside. What would it matter if the lass was comely or ugly?

"Nay."

Colman pursed his lips. His cheeks were hollow, and deep grooves ran from his nose to his chin. A weak chin, Gormach thought, and a thin, cruel mouth.

"You have the payment?" Colman asked.

Gormach slipped the knot on the small leather sack tied to his belt. He handed the sack to Colman. "The remainder will be sent the day after the marriage."

Colman cradled the sack in his palm, assessing its weight. "You swear to this marriage?"

Gormach gritted his teeth. "I, Gormach mac Nechtan mac Aed, chief of Strath Erne in the land of the Picts, whose son is the grandson of Oengus, do swear to this marriage."

He could not resist mentioning Oengus. The man had slaughtered the Irish on their own land.

Colman's eyes flashed briefly before his lips flattened into a rigid smile. "And our clans shall be friends?"

"So the Danes will think."

The smile disappeared. A slight glow of satisfaction warmed Gormach's belly. He was not so old that he had forgotten how to make men wary.

"I will send her within the fortnight." Abruptly, Colman turned and strode away, his footsteps grinding the sand.

Gormach kept his eyes on the Irishman until he was swallowed up by the mist. Even then, he stared into the shrouded distance as a hardening drizzle coated his face. Gormach pulled air deeply into his lungs before letting it shudder out. He was tired, he realized, and very wet and cold. He longed for his own mountains.

My God in heaven, he prayed, *give us strength.*

His heart heavy in his chest, he trudged to his curach and pushed off into the sea.

Chapter Two

Mhoire lifted her face to the wind. God's breath. She closed her eyes and let the cool air stream against her skin. The wind was full of power. It pressed hard against her eyelids and flattened her hair against her cheek. Perhaps, if she could sit still for just a moment, it would smooth out the thumping of her heart and the fluttering in her stomach.

"Lady." An impatient voice broke her reverie. Nay, she could not remain long on this mountaintop. She must move forward. She must gather her courage and start a new life.

She glanced at the man sitting on the stallion beside her. His face was unreadable, just as it had been for the last three days, ever since he and his men had met her and Grainne on the beach when they stepped from her father's curach. But Mhoire didn't need an expression to know what the man was thinking. He despised her. They all did. Every one of these half-dozen Picts who rode in near-silence, bristling with weapons.

She lifted her hand to the soft leather pouch that hung below her breast and fingered the objects she carried there. Then she squeezed her mare's flanks and rode slowly forward.

This island of the Picts, the Britons, and the Scots was close to the island of Ireland, just a few hours in the curach across the channel, and yet it looked so different. The first day, the men had rowed them up the most enormous loch Mhoire had ever seen. And then they had come upon these

4

mountains—the great spine that separated the western coast
from the land of the Picts. Here clouds bunched against the
peaks in rolling masses, and slender rivulets of water
poured down the steep crags like shards of shining metal.

They rode across a plateau covered with dark green
heather until they came upon one of the huge standing
stones that Mhoire knew were scattered all across Pictland.
The stone slab was as tall as she was, twice as thick as a
man's arm, and densely carved. The Irish called the Picts
Cruithne—people of the designs—and now Mhoire understood why. She picked out images of a boar, a falcon, a
half-moon, and a lightning rod. The designs, she knew,
recorded marriage treaties and described the lineage of the
clan that lived in the area. They gave a warning, too: This
clan was as strong as a boar, as swift to kill as a falcon, as
intelligent as the moon, and as deadly as lightning.

Soon the plateau fell away, and a broad glen lay open
before them. Orderly fields and pastures spread from one
side to the other. Horses grazed on tender, yellow-green
grasses, and long strips of newly dug black earth gleamed
with fertility.

Suddenly, laughter erupted. For the first time since
Mhoire had come under their guard, the men were relaxed
on their horses, and their faces were animated.

This must be their home.

She squared her shoulders and sat as tall as she could on
her horse. She prayed. *Mother of God. Mother of God.
Mother of God.*

The hillfort rose from the floor of the glen. It looked like
the forts of Ireland—a knobby hill wrapped with a series
of fortifications. Mhoire knew that inside the outer stone
wall would be an inner courtyard holding a main gathering
hall and smaller buildings made of turf and stone. Circling
the top was a second line of defense with three warriors
stationed as sentries. *These Picts are careful,* Mhoire
thought to herself. But then, everyone was these days.

They passed thatch-roofed cottages outside the fort and

rode through the gate. Inside, the clan was gathered to witness her arrival, and a sea of distrustful eyes fastened on her small person. A low babble rose from the assembly like the rustling of leaves on a stormy day. Children held tightly to their mothers' skirts.

She slipped to the ground and smoothed the folds of her tunic. She wore a plain woolen garment, which she had dyed a soft rose color with lichen. A plain leather belt circled her waist. Mhoire had chosen the garment to travel in because it was practical—warm and sturdy. But now she wished she had on something that more suited the daughter of a provincial king.

A calloused hand slipped into the crook of her arm. Grainne. Mhoire turned and smiled weakly, taking comfort in her friend's lean, familiar face and steady gaze.

"Do you see him?" Grainne whispered.

"Who?"

"The Pict who wants to marry you. Do you see him?"

Tentatively, Mhoire scanned the crowd, hoping one face would somehow distinguish itself.

"Nay . . ."

"*There!*" Grainne squeezed Mhoire's arm.

The crowd was moving to left and right, like a stream of water flowing to each side of a rock. A man emerged.

Mhoire's blood froze.

He was old—at least as old as her father, with gray hair that hung to his chin like an animal's pelt. Tall and broad, he looked as unyielding as a rock. He wore a long ceremonial tunic of fine gray wool, and a thick, golden torc circled his neck. On the left side of his face a jagged scar ran from his forehead to his chin.

Mhoire met his eyes. They were unyielding as well, and as cold as the North Sea. Surely, she told herself, her father had not betrothed her to this one.

The crowd hushed.

Perhaps they were waiting for her to bow her head and bend her knee, Mhoire thought. She remained standing.

The man gave her a long, considering look. "You'll be

wanting a meal, lass," he stated finally. As the crowd watched silently, she followed him into the gathering hall.

She sat with Grainne and the gray-haired man at one end of a long wooden table that was heaped with platters. The men who had brought them here were seated at the other end of the table, where they were tearing into the food. Straw covered the dirt floor, and a small fire burned in the center of the room. Weapons hung from pegs on the walls—row upon row of leather shields, iron spears, and throwing axes. They caught the flickering light of the flames, and seemed to dance like living things.

Mhoire wanted to run, but she knew that was the coward's way out. Ever since she was a girl, she had been told the stories of the Morrigan, the women warriors of Ireland who could slay men and beasts with their magic weapons. They would not run. Nay, they would overwhelm every man in this room. Inwardly, Mhoire sighed. She didn't have magic weapons, not even her own bow—it was somewhere with her baggage. But she could at least contain her fear.

She slipped her eating dagger from the leather sheath on her belt and picked at a piece of turnip in the wooden trencher that had been set before her.

"What is your name, lass?" the gray-haired man asked, as he stabbed a piece of venison with his dagger.

"I am Mhoire. Mhoire ni Colman."

He nodded as he bit into the venison. With cautious glances, Mhoire studied his face. His features were well-proportioned and strong, his nose long and straight, his forehead high, and his eyes deeply set under wiry dark gray brows. But the scar that ran down the left side of his face ruined him. From the looks of it, his cheek had nearly been cleaved open. Like most women of responsibility, Mhoire had often stitched wounds, and she could see that no one had stitched this one. It had healed itself on its own as best it could, into an ugly, irregular, white ridge of flesh.

Suddenly he looked up. In his eyes she saw a sadness so

deep it pricked her heart. But in a blink it was gone, and his eyes dulled to an unreadable gray.

He leaned back in his chair.

"My son may change his attitude about marriage once he sees you."

"Your son?"

"Drosten. The man you are to marry."

She breathed a silent prayer of relief. "Your son is Drosten? Then you are . . ."

One side of his mouth tugged upward. "Did you think you were to marry me, lass?"

She smiled wanly. "You must be Gormach."

"Aye. You have heard of me."

"I have heard much of you." *Ruthless,* was the word the harpers used when they sang of Gormach mac Nechtan.

"Drosten is away. Killing a few Britons." Gormach picked up his goblet and took a prolonged swallow of ale.

"So the wedding will be some time from now?"

Gormach shrugged. "Tomorrow. Perhaps the next day. As soon as Drosten returns."

Mhoire felt the color drain from her face. "So soon?"

"As soon as possible. No sense in delaying, lass."

Mhoire laid her dagger next to the trencher and gripped her hands in her lap. The noise of the men eating and talking at the other end of the table hammered in her ears.

She looked up. Gormach's eyes narrowed. "We cannot wait. You understand the situation, lass?"

She took a deep breath. "I know you wish an alliance between the Picts and the Irish." *Be calm. Be strong.*

"We *wish* nothing. We *need* an alliance, and we need it most with the Scots. If we get the Irish, too, as part of the bargain, so much the better. But I do not give a pig's fart about the Irish."

The entire hall went silent, except for the fire, which sizzled and snapped.

"I am Irish," Mhoire murmured.

"Nay, you are not."

"What do you mean?"

"Your father has given you Dun Darach—your mother's family land in Dal Riata. That makes you a Scot." Gormach reached for another slab of venison. "When you marry my son you will do so as a Scot."

Mhoire didn't understand. She was the daughter of an Irish king—not a high king but still a man of some stature. Yet Gormach was more interested in the fact that her mother had been a Scot. It was true Mhoire was bringing to the marriage a holding in Dal Riata, but why was that more important than being an Irish princess?

"You hate the Irish," she stated flatly.

"I don't hate the Irish, lass. But I don't trust them. I don't trust any people whose sons I have killed on the battlefield—the Irish, the Britons." He swallowed the meat. "There is only one people that I hate."

"The Danes?"

He nodded.

Why do men fight so much? The enmity between the Picts and the Britons was legendary. The Britons lived just to the south of Pictland, and for hundreds of years the two peoples had fought territorial wars. As for the Danes, they were everyone's enemy, burning hillforts and fields up and down the coasts of all the northern seas. But why? Why does one country invade another? Why not live peacefully in one's own land?

"So you hate the Danes, and you mistrust everyone else."

"Aye."

"Including my father?"

"In particular, your father."

"Why?"

"Because my wife's father, Oengus, invaded your country and slaughtered your clan, and yet your father is willing to marry you to my son. Your father does not strike me as a forgiving man."

That was true enough. Her father did not know the meaning of forgiveness, or any other charitable impulse.

"I do not know my father's motives, but one might guess

they are the same as yours. We, too, are troubled by the Danes and could benefit from having an ally against them."

Gormach grunted and continued eating.

Everyone else returned to their food as well. Mhoire picked up her dagger and probed a piece of venison. A serving woman placed a platter of salmon at Mhoire's elbow. Cooked whole, the fish's damp scales glistened, and their empty black eyes shone.

Mhoire cleared her throat. "I don't understand why you favor the Scots. They are Irish people."

Gormach peered at her over the salmon. "They *were* Irish. But they left Ireland ten generations ago to settle in Dal Riata. No one considers them Irish now. They are Dal Riata Scots."

"But you have fought with the Scots, too," she persisted. "Oengus also invaded Dal Riata and then the Scots rallied and threw him out, killing many Pictish warriors."

Gormach grabbed his goblet and thumped it on the table. The salmon bounced. The hall lapsed into silence. From somewhere under the table, a dog whined.

"What is your point, lass?"

"My point—" she barely managed to keep her voice steady—"is that since the Dal Riata Scots really are no different than the Britons or the Irish, you should not be allying yourself with them. You should be looking for other solutions to this problem with the Danes."

Gormach's face reddened.

"You could unite your provinces," she continued. "That would be the sensible thing to do. All the Pictish kings could fight together. Surely, a united Pictland would overcome any invading force."

Gormach's anger burst. "Are you daft, lass? We are being attacked on all sides—the Britons from the south and the Danes from the east and the west and the north. We need land in Dal Riata. We need Dun Darach. We need an ally on the west coast. We need the hillfort there and strong defenses."

Mhoire clenched her hands together in her lap. Her

nerves were frayed, and the smell of the fish was making her queasy. "But you have no reason to trust the Scots, your former enemy, any more than the Irish or the Britons. This doesn't make sense."

"Lass, we have no need to *trust* the Scots. Trust plays no part here. We have you. And once you—a Scot, thanks to your Scottish mother—marry my son, you will be a Pict. And Dun Darach, your land, will be ours."

Now. She must speak now. Mhoire took another shaking breath and looked straight into his hot, hard eyes. "I regret to tell you that you cannot have me."

Gormach's eyes narrowed. "I do not understand your meaning."

She broke into a cold sweat. "I mean that your agreement with my father was a terrible mistake. I have here . . ." She fumbled with the small pouch hanging from her neck. ". . . I have here the gold you gave my father." With unsteady fingers, she loosened the drawstring, pulled out a gold medallion, and laid it on the table. It was as large as a child's palm and heavily engraved.

Gormach stared at it, his face flaming, except for the scar, which remained a dead-white gash.

"This is yours, is it not? I am returning it to you."

Gormach lifted burning eyes to hers. "Put her under guard," he said.

Chapter Three

Drosten unbelted his scabbard and leaned it against the wall of the cistern. In one quick move, he pulled his short tunic over his head and flung it onto the ground. Bending over, he peeled off his leather boots and kicked them out of the way.

He was hot and dirty, crusted with bog mud and a fair amount of his own blood. The blood was from flesh wounds only, fortunately. He didn't even glance at them, but thrust his muscled legs over the side of the wooden tub. With a splash, he sank into the cool waters.

It had been a trying day. First, there had been the hard ride home. A courier had found him on the southern plains and announced that his marriage had been arranged and he was to return immediately to Strath Erne. Dutifully, Drosten had pressed his horse and his men so that he would arrive when his father expected. Then, the moment he had gotten through the gates, before he was even off his horse, he discovered that his bride had refused him. Drosten closed his eyes and leaned back. He felt a tightening in his gut whenever he thought of it. *Refused him.* It reminded him of the woman who had spurned him years before. Only this Irishwoman—this Scot, as his father insisted on calling her—hadn't even laid eyes on him.

Damnation, he had bad luck with women! But this one wouldn't get away, he knew that. It was unthinkable.

Whether she liked it or not—whether *he* liked it or not—the marriage must take place.

Drosten reached for the straw brush and the slab of lye soap that sat on the cistern wall. With rough strokes, he lathered up the brush and began scrubbing his powerful arms.

He had been fighting the Britons along the border. If you could call what those cowards did fighting. The Britons had the courage of children—they attacked in the woods and scarcely ever came out in the open to stand their ground. They did, however, occasionally kill a few men. None of his, though. Drosten prided himself that of all the Picts who led men into battle, he was the most canny. It was a matter of keeping your head on your shoulders and not letting your enemy lure you into the woods where you could be separated and slaughtered one by one. Aye, fighting was simple, as long as you used your brain.

A lot simpler than dealing with women.

Drosten immersed his arms in the water to rinse off the soap, and then attacked his neck with the brush.

Why him? Why did he have to marry the woman? His mother was the daughter of a queen and that put him in the royal line, making him a candidate for king of one of the seven Pictish provinces. Of course, there were plenty of other candidates. His mother's eldest brother—Drosten's uncle—was king now. And when his uncle died, there were two of his uncle's brothers to choose from plus the sons of his mother's two sisters. When the time came, a committee would choose. It was this ability—indeed, mandate—to withhold the crown from a weak inheritor and bestow it upon the ablest royal man that had kept the Picts strong for generation after generation.

Drosten knew that many considered him to be the best choice. He was a good leader and the province needed a leader.

Instead, the clan had told him to do this.

He applied the brush to his chest. The soap ate at the half-healed cuts and made his skin sting.

Marry this woman with the holding in Dal Riata, his father and uncles had commanded. Leave Pictland and everyone you know and go to the fort called Dun Darach. Create a fighting force out of anyone who was available and protect the western coast at all costs.

Drosten lathered his big hands and scoured his face, digging with his fingernails to loosen the caked mud.

And, by the way, they said, have plenty of children with this woman who doesn't even want to get near you.

He spit some soap out of his mouth. This task made chasing the Britons seem as easy as catching a new-born kitten. Women! What a bother they were. Drosten rubbed the soap through his hair. He much preferred the company of men. But this was his duty, his obligation to his clan. Never would he have considered refusing to do what his family asked.

He laid the brush carefully on the edge of the cistern, took a breath, and plunged completely under the water.

"So what is the plan now?" Grainne asked.

"I'm thinking of one," Mhoire answered. "Just give me a few more moments."

They were sitting side by side on a small pallet in the tiny windowless hut in which they had been imprisoned since the day before. Only once had the door opened to let in a stooped old crone, wrapped in a plaid shawl, with a bowl of fresh water in her hands and a loaf of bannoch under her arm. The woman had given them that hostile, piercing look that Mhoire was beginning to associate with all Picts, deposited the food, and left.

A plan. In truth, Mhoire had a plan, though it wasn't working very well—to claim Dun Darach for herself. No husband, no marriage, just a quiet life on her mother's land.

"They have this idea that you have to marry one of them. They're not going to let you back out of it."

"Aye, I know. But there's no logic to it. I'm giving them back their gold, and they don't like us, no matter what they say. Surely, another woman would do as well, don't you think?"

Grainne's brows drew together. "They want Dun Darach very badly. As much as you. And your father promised it. That's logic enough for them."

Mhoire lowered her head and felt the cold spot in her stomach spread wider.

Dun Darach—"Fort of the Oaks." To Mhoire's mind, the words carried the heft and rhythm of poetry. She had said them to herself so many times, they were like a prayer that inspired her and comforted her when nothing else could. Dun Darach. She was sure it must be strong, welcoming, and beautiful beyond all imagining.

The truth was she knew very little about the place. On this subject, her mother, never very talkative, had been entirely mute. Mhoire knew that Eveline was the daughter of a Scottish chieftain and had left Dun Darach as a young woman to marry Colman and live in Ireland. But that was all.

And then, at the last quarter moon, all opportunity for learning more disappeared. Her mother took ill after supper, complaining of a sour stomach. Mhoire brewed comfrey tea and helped her into bed. Sometime during the night, Eveline died.

Then yesterweek Colman told Mhoire he had arranged her marriage and her mother's land was to be her marriage gift. *The Picts are keen for it,* he had hissed with a gleam in his eye. *They need an alliance against the Danes.* Mhoire didn't care two twigs what the Picts needed. As soon as Colman had said the words "Dun Darach," she wanted it.

She had spent the next days preparing. She packed her bags with seed that she stole from the granary, dried apples, two loaves of bannoch, a large bag of oats, an iron pot and trivet, and as many arrows as she had time to make. That left room for only a few pieces of clothing and some medicinal herbs. She prayed that her father wouldn't look inside her bags. But then, even if he had, she doubted he would guess what she was plotting. Until that moment, she had never been a rebellious daughter. Just a lonely one, determined not to live her mother's life.

She was afraid of the Picts, she had to admit that. The harpers sang of men as big as giants and as tenacious as Satan himself. The Picts, they said, paralyzed their enemies with their battle cries. Their weapons grew large in their hands, and their arrows never missed their targets. And, the harpers told, if a spear pierced the body of a Pict, it crumbled and turned to dust.

What could one small Irishwoman mean to them? Mhoire had reasoned. Her father had little prominence in Ireland. As much as he yearned for glory, he had never gained the respect of the high king or even of the lesser chieftains over whom he theoretically reigned. Surely, the Picts could find another, more noble woman to take into their clan. Indeed, she had convinced herself that once she returned their fabulous golden brooch, she could simply leave their inland fort and retrace her steps to the western coast and Dun Darach. She could put the past behind her and take charge of her own destiny.

Now she realized how foolish she had been.

"How did you get the gold brooch from your father?"

Mhoire sighed. "I stole it from his bedchamber the night before we left. He was so ale-headed that he fell asleep with it right beside him on the coverlet."

"He will be furious when he discovers it is gone."

"Aye."

Mhoire turned to her friend. Grainne had not been forced to accompany her. The day her father had declared the betrothal, Mhoire had confided her plans to Grainne, and Grainne had offered to come. She, too, wanted to live somewhere other than in a small Irish province over which dark clouds of misery always seemed to hang.

Mhoire knew Grainne was eager to avoid her own marriage, which was to take place that spring to a rough Irish farmer with the brains of a fish. Grainne deserved better. She held no stature in the clan, and she was not very pretty, that was true. Her hair was a dull brown, her skin tended toward sallow, and her body was so loosely put together it appeared as shapeless as a sack half full of oats. But Grainne's eyes shone with a deep and keen thoughtfulness and a loyalty that was as strong as iron.

"I am sorry this has happened, Grainne. But I do not want a married life. I want to live in my own way, in peace. You understand, don't you?"

"Aye."

"So we must do something. We can't just sit here."

"We could pray."

Mhoire nodded. "Aye. Perhaps God will help us."

The women slipped onto their knees. For long moments, neither moved, each intent on her pleas. Then Mhoire lifted her face. Slowly, her attention focused on a corner of the hut where the wall met the thatched roof. A gauzy beam of light shimmered through the thatching.

"Grainne!" she whispered. "Look at the roof!"

"Where? What do you see?"

Mhoire rose and stepped over to the wall. On tiptoes, she probed the thatch.

"There's a hole here."

Grainne came up behind her. "You're certain?"

"Aye." Mhoire reached under her tunic and pulled out a knife. The Picts had taken their eating daggers but had neglected to look under her skirts for the larger one with the stout bone handle that she kept strapped to her leg. "The rope holding down this part of the roof must have loosened."

She sliced out a chunk of thatch. The opening wasn't large, but they could wiggle through.

"Here is our plan." She turned to Grainne. "We will climb out and find the stable and a horse and, please God, my bow and arrows."

"And the guard? What about him?"

"He's on the other side of the hut. He won't see us."

"And once you have your bow, you can fight off any man who pursues us."

Mhoire's spirit lifted. "Aye. Then we'll ride out of here."

"You know the way to Dun Darach?"

Mhoire paused. She didn't. Neither she nor Grainne had ever been outside of her father's holding, let alone in this country. "I know the holding is on the west coast." Her mind raced. "We'll head west, back over the mountains, and make inquiries along the way."

Grainne seemed satisfied with the answer, and Mhoire turned to face the wall. She could just get her boot in between the timbers. Grasping her knife between her teeth, she started climbing.

In a moment, she was peeping through the roof. They were near the outer edge of the hillfort. Below was a large cistern filled with water, but no one seemed to be near.

She snaked through the hole. Gripping the ropes that held down the thatch, she dangled her feet over the roof's edge and dropped lightly to the ground.

The splash from the cistern behind her made her turn abruptly.

Mother of God!

A man's head was rising from the water.

Mhoire gasped, and her knife clattered to the ground.

He opened his eyes and let out his breath at the same time. Surprise skittered across his face.

Then he started to stand.

Mhoire panicked at the sight of his emerging nakedness. "Nay! Nay! Nay!" she pleaded. She squeezed her eyes shut and held out her arms.

A tense silence followed.

The guard's footsteps pattered around the corner. *Her knife!* She opened her eyes and lunged for it.

"Don't."

The naked man's voice was low and deep.

Mhoire froze, half-crouched. Out of the corner of her eye, she saw the guard stop as well.

She heard sloshing.

"Who are you?" the man asked.

Hesitantly, Mhoire rose, turning toward him at the same time. She glimpsed his muscled body streaming with water.

Light glinted off a large, heavy sword, which he held in his hand. She squeezed her eyes shut again.

"You know who I am."

"Nay. I do not."

"Then you are the only person in this hillfort who is so ignorant."

"Apparently so."

Mhoire steadied herself. "I am Mhoire ni Colman."

"You?" She could hear the astonishment in his voice.

"Aye. Don't I look like an Irishwoman to you? Don't I have some . . . some loathsome feature that distinguishes me from a Pict? That makes me look peculiar and hateful? Everyone else in this fort seems to recognize me easily enough."

Desperation was making her angry.

She sensed the guard move. Fear rose in her chest, and, flinging her eyes open again, she lunged for the knife. But the guard was retreating around the corner of the hut.

"I wish you would leave that knife alone."

Mhoire stilled in a half-crouch. "And I wish you would clothe yourself so that I could look at the person to whom I am speaking."

The water splashed heavily. Frowning, she held her position, trying to judge whether she could reach the knife before he could reach her. Perhaps. But his sword would be no match for her small weapon.

"You can look at me now."

Reluctantly, Mhoire stood and faced him. He had gotten out of the cistern and put on a coarse, dun-colored tunic. Now he was watching her thoughtfully.

His hair was the color of wet sand, a mixture of gold and brown that gleamed brightly in the sunlight. Water dripped from the locks sticking to his brow and streamed down his face onto a strong neck. He was a tall man, Mhoire noticed immediately, with broad shoulders and long, muscled limbs.

His demeanor told her he was a warrior. Barefoot, his body slick with water, he exuded the kind of physical confidence that men gained only after years of battle and a harsh life spent outdoors. He bristled with wariness, too—the wariness of a warrior whose first task was to appraise the enemy.

They locked eyes. His were dark blue, the color of the mountains that surrounded them.

"I knew you weren't a Pict, that is true." He leaned his sword against the side of the cistern and folded his arms across his chest.

Mhoire tensed. "And how is that?"

"Pictish women usually leave a building through the door and not the roof."

His eyes went from her to the roof and back to her head. Instinctively, Mhoire lifted her hand to her hair. She could feel coarse strands of thatch stuck in it. *Mother of God! She must be a sight.* She grimaced. She hated being laughed at.

"I use a door when it has not been barred," she said, stiffening her back. "I take the roof rather than remain captive against my will."

He lifted an eyebrow and nodded. His assessing gaze reached into her soul and made her squirm.

"And you, sir," she continued, her irritation mounting. "What are you going to do? Everyone here is treating me like a prisoner. You have me cornered. Will you throw me back in the trap? Will you, too, force a woman to do what she does not wish?"

Something shifted in his face. His eyes hardened, and he unfolded his arms. Every nerve in Mhoire's body leapt.

"I must," he answered quietly.

He stood unmoving, four paces from her. But his presence was suddenly as hot as peat fire.

Mhoire looked into his dark eyes and found she could not look away. In that instant she realized who he was.

Chapter Four

Drosten called for the guard and told him to move Mhoire and Grainne from the hut in which they were imprisoned and into his own sleeping chamber. He also ordered the man to guard the door. The women deserved more comfort, but he was not so foolish as to believe they would stay put.

He was careful to show nothing but resolve during these proceedings, but inwardly he found himself smiling. The Irishwoman seemed inordinately disconcerted that she was caught with her hair tangled. And what a sight she was— her face flushed, her eyes flashing, her small body drawn to its full height and trembling with indignation, and that cascade of dark hair studded with straw. Now, walking purposefully toward the gathering hall, Drosten grinned.

He sobered quickly when Alfred fell into step beside him.

"You've seen your bride, then?"

"News runs as fleet as a hare around here," Drosten muttered.

"When you house a prisoner in your own sleeping chamber, everyone is curious."

Drosten's frown deepened. "She's the daughter of a king. We can't treat her like a common thief."

Alfred eyed Drosten closely but said nothing. The men had been friends since they were both old enough to hold a weapon. In coloring, Alfred was Drosten's opposite—

dark-eyed and dark-haired. But like Drosten, he was un-married. The son of a common clansman, Alfred seemed content with a soldier's life—perhaps, Drosten often sur-mised, because it kept him unencumbered of a wife.

The two walked for a moment in silence, falling into the same stride.

Everyone, Drosten realized, must know what had tran-spired. That roused his irritation.

"What are you going to do with her, then?"

Drosten groaned and stopped dead in his tracks.

"I'm going to marry her. Do you doubt that?"

Alfred puckered his lips.

Drosten turned away and continued walking toward the hall.

"You could do with a cup of ale, my friend." Alfred clapped him on the back. "It would clear your mind."

The gathering hall was empty, except for a few dogs stretched out on their sides, sleeping. A hazy half-light, cast by a beam of sunlight that streamed through the hole in the ceiling above the hearth, bathed the interior. The noon meal had been eaten hours before, and it being a rare sunny day, the women were down by the stream washing clothes and laying them on the grass to dry. A large kettle of broth—the beginnings of supper—simmered unattended over a low fire.

Drosten was grateful not to have to face inquisitive looks. Stepping to a heavy oak sideboard, he and Alfred poured themselves beakers of ale from a bronze jug, and then strolled toward the long table in the center of the room, drinking thirstily as they went.

They sat down opposite each other.

"You think she'll come around, then?" Alfred asked over the rim of his beaker.

"Nay, I don't."

"So what will you do?"

Drosten ignored the question to ask one of his own. "Did she say anything to my father about why she is resisting?"

"Well, what I've heard is that she told him he was going about the entire affair the wrong way, and that he should solve his problems by uniting the provinces instead of marrying his son to his enemies."

Drosten smiled. "Did she now? Brave woman."

"It's a wonder your father didn't slice her to bits and eat her for supper."

Drosten's smile broadened. "I can just see her fighting back with that dagger of hers. Who let her keep that?"

Alfred shook his head. "Must have hidden it up her shift, the little weasel."

"Up her shift?" A part of Drosten wanted to give that thought full consideration, but his more rational self refused. The last thing he was about to do was let a woman bewitch him.

"You're interested in this woman, aren't you?"

As quickly as he had smiled, Drosten scowled. "It's my duty to marry her, and, by God in heaven, I will." He shoved himself away from the table and headed across the room toward the sideboard.

"Hmm." Alfred took another swallow of ale. A few seconds passed. One of the dogs groaned in his sleep. "She's a peculiar female."

"She's a stubborn female."

"Not like Fionna."

Drosten's grip tightened on the jug but he managed to pour the ale without spilling a drop. Few people dared speak Fionna's name in his presence. The ale must be loosening Alfred's tongue.

When Drosten settled himself on the bench again, his face was as blank as a clear mountain loch.

He had intended to say nothing, but the words slipped from his mouth. "She seems very like Fionna to me."

"Nay, man, think on it. Fionna lied as easily as a squirrel runs. This one, even though she's been devious with her father, has been honest with us. Stupidly so, if you ask me."

Drosten considered Alfred's statement. "She is honest, isn't she?"

"If I were you, you know what I would do?"

Drosten lifted an eyebrow.

"I'd throw her over my shoulder and haul her to the priest before this day was over."

"Alfred, my friend, even if you were the bonniest warrior in the province, you'd never get on with a woman that way."

"And you know a better method for dealing with a bull-headed bride?"

Drosten drained his beaker and stood. "I think I'll have a talk with her."

"A talk?" Alfred's mouth fell open as he watched his friend head for the door. "You think you know how to talk with a woman?"

"Nay." Drosten looked back from the threshold. "But I know how to wage a war. And that's what we have here."

Drosten's sleeping chamber was sparsely furnished, but it did contain elements of comfort. The most prominent was the woven rug that covered most of the stone floor. It had been dyed a dark purple, and the moment Mhoire and Grainne had entered the room, they had gazed at it in wonder. Purple dye, made from whelks, was rare and highly valued; to have a rug of that hue signaled wealth and prestige. The Picts, Mhoire knew, were a sea-faring people who traveled far to trade with other countries. Their excursions had obviously brought them riches.

On one side of the chamber was a planked sleeping platform covered with a mattress that had been newly filled with heather. A low wooden chest stood along the opposite wall, and a full leather pack sat unceremoniously by the door. By the worn look of it, Mhoire guessed it was Drosten's. Likely he had dumped it there earlier, not expecting to be giving over his sleeping chamber to two women.

One long window, its leather covering pulled back, occupied the far wall, and it was there that Mhoire stood, gazing down the broad cleft of the glen. Puffy clouds drifted across the sun, and light and shadow dappled the countryside. In the fields, she could see dozens of men scattering seed. With the grace born of repetitive labor, they reached into the bags slung over their shoulders and then flung out their arms in wide arcs. Mhoire was too far away to see the seed itself, but she knew the silky feel of it, the promise of its weight in the hand. She loved sowing seed. Sometimes she thought that the only happy times she had ever had in her father's fort were those spring days when every able person took to the fields to help plant the year's crop. Now she ached to be on her own land, planting life and hope.

Instead, she was wrapped in worry.

The knock on the door made her jump. She turned.

Drosten filled the doorway. He paused for just a moment, and then took a few steps in, closing the door behind him. Suddenly, the room seemed tiny.

He fixed his gaze on Mhoire. "I would like a word with you."

She inclined her head. She wanted a chance to make her arguments. But she remained by the window, thinking that if the situation became dire, she could jump out of it.

He took his time looking at her, so she looked at him in turn. His hair had dried to the color of spun gold, and it was so tousled she concluded he must have combed it with his fingers. His ears were exposed, and she was surprised to note how delicate they were, well-shaped and not overly large, and flat against his head with silky threads of golden hair curling around them. They seemed to belie the rest of him, which radiated a rough strength that Mhoire realized had an unsettling capacity to fluster her.

Grainne moved to her side. If she had been a dog, she would have been growling.

"I won't hurt anyone," Drosten stated.

Neither woman responded.

Sighing heavily, Drosten pulled a dagger from under his belt and held it out to Mhoire, hilt first. She recognized the bone handle.

"Take it."

She lifted her eyes to his face, but his expression revealed nothing of his motives. Craving the tiny bit of protection her weapon provided, she slowly reached out. His hand was as large as the rest of him, brown from the sun, with long, capable fingers. As she grasped the dagger, her fingers grazed his. They were firm, callused, and warm. She felt a shock when she touched them, and quickly pulled back.

At Mhoire's nod, Grainne slipped out of the room.

Drosten gestured toward the bed with his chin. "Please, sit."

She shook her head. He towered over her as it was.

Drosten sighed again and lowered himself onto the chest. "As you choose."

An awkward silence ensued. Mhoire had expected anger, perhaps even violence. Not this utterly calm reserve.

She cleared her throat. "You wished a word with me?"

He nodded.

"Well?" she prompted.

Drosten folded his arms across his broad chest. Mhoire noticed that he was still wearing the dirty tunic he had pulled on after he climbed out of his bath. All his clean clothes were here, in his sleeping chamber, she realized. Acutely aware of the intimacy of the setting, she blushed furiously.

"I would like you to explain your actions." His voice, tinged with a Pictish accent, was as serene as if he were talking about the weather. His eyes, however, were penetrating.

She looked down at the dagger. How could she tell her story in a way that he would understand? How could she possibly explain how much Dun Darach meant to her? And why should he care?

He won't care. That's the truth of it. No one gives a mare's tail for a woman's desires.

Desperately, she cast about for the right words, the convincing words.

She attempted to match his equanimity. "Your clan

would be wiser to align more closely with the clans of the other Pictish provinces than to attempt friendship with an old enemy."

"Perhaps," he conceded. "But since we haven't managed it yet, I doubt we could manage it now. Oftentimes it is easier to bed with a stranger than a relative."

Mhoire's face flamed again. His analogy was far too apt. One argument gone. She tried another.

"I am only the daughter of a very minor king. Given your rank . . ." She gestured vaguely with the hand that held the dagger. ". . . you could marry a woman in a much higher position."

He nodded. "Aye, I could."

"Why don't you?"

"My clan has asked me to do this."

"But why? Why me? I don't understand. You could have any woman."

"Not every woman has Dun Darach."

Dun Darach. The words stabbed at her heart. She willed herself to maintain control. Still, her voice filled with emotion.

"Why do you want it so much?" she asked.

He looked at her with intense curiosity. "We need to defend the coast from the Danes. It's as simple as that. Why do you want it?"

She looked down again, blinking her eyes and running her thumb along the smooth bone of the dagger's handle. Tears were close, but she would not allow him to see them.

When she had regained her composure, she met his gaze. "I want to have a life there. My own life."

His eyes hardened. "None of us has our own life."

The words cut her to the bone. He spoke the truth. And the truth shattered all her fragile dreams.

Mhoire turned and faced the window. She rested the dagger on the ledge, gripped her hands together, and rested them there as well. Waves of sadness broke over her. Fear, despair, and an unnamable emptiness—all the emotions she had carried for so many years—pressed on her shoulders.

All she wanted was a bit of land. Surely that was not so much to ask for. She stared at the fields, tried to focus on the men who were sowing seed. But they were farther away now, and she could barely make out their forms.

She was aware of Drosten rising and stepping toward her, but she was too burdened by grief to feel endangered. At that moment, he could have cut off her head and she wouldn't have cared.

"What kind of life did you imagine?" His voice was surprisingly gentle.

"I thought . . ." Her voice shook. She could hear it and she hated it. She drew a tremulous breath and tried again. "I wanted . . . I wanted an ordinary life. I brought seed . . ." She could not stop the waver. *Mother of God, don't let me cry!*

He waited for her to continue, but she could not.

"You thought to do this alone?" he probed.

She nodded. Discreetly, she hoped, she wiped the tears from her eyes with the back of her hand. "You think that it is foolish for a woman to live on her holding alone?"

"I think it is unusual and very dangerous."

Mhoire prickled at that. She turned to face him. He was near. Very near, and watching her closely. Her heartbeat quickened.

"I can protect myself."

He glanced at the dagger lying on the window ledge. "You would need more than that."

She lifted her chin. "I have other weapons, and I know how to use them."

An eyebrow went up. His brows were very fine, she noticed. A shade of golden brown darker than his hair.

"You would fight off a thousand men, then?"

"If I had to." Her voice was firmer now. "I would try." He looked skeptical.

"Do you know Scathach?" she asked.

He shook his head.

"Scathach was the greatest teacher of warriors in the world. She taught Cuchulain the secrets of battle. How to hurl a spear, how to sight an arrow from three hundred paces, how to leap over his enemies, how to scream until men fainted. Scathach was a woman, and she could fight better than any man."

Drosten's mouth turned down. "If you believe yourself as strong as Scathach, you will be killed within a fortnight."

Mhoire's spine snapped straight. She opened her mouth as if to blurt a reply, but thought better of it and pressed her lips together. In her experience, men were not capable of acknowledging a woman's strength.

Running his hand through his hair, Drosten turned away and took a few steps toward the center of the room. When he faced her, his jaw was set in a determined line.

"Your father made an agreement with my clan."

Reluctantly, Mhoire nodded.

"You expected us to allow you to break it."

She could see anger sparkling in his eyes. "I believed that if I returned to you what was yours, we could sever the agreement."

He put his hands on his hips. "Tell me this. Do women ever keep their promises?"

"I myself made no promise."

"No promise? No promise, you say? My father risked his life to travel to Ireland. Your father gave his word you would be delivered to us. And Dun Darach, too."

Mhoire stood immobile, afraid to say a word that might ignite a rage whose consequences she could not predict. She watched Drosten struggle to contain himself, and was relieved to see him succeed.

"Did the Danes ever attack your father's fort?" he finally asked.

She shook her head.

"Well, let me tell you what it is like. They descend like a fire from the sky, burning fields, homes, haystacks, everything in sight. They slaughter every man—old, sick, enfeebled, it doesn't matter. Then they gather the women and children, and that's when they have their sport. The women are raped, in full sight of the young ones, by man after man, and if they don't die from it, they're herded onto dragonships and brought back to Daneland as slaves. As for the children . . ." His voice stumbled and recovered. "The children are enslaved as well, or they are left, to survive as best they can."

Mhoire paled. "I'm sorry," she whispered.

In the space between them, horrific images danced.

"Surely you can see that we must stop them."

Mhoire bowed her head and said nothing.

Drosten blew out an exasperated breath and ran his hand through his hair. He began pacing the room. Despite his anger, Mhoire no longer felt threatened, at least not physically. If he had been inclined to use force, he wouldn't be spending this much time talking to her. She wondered why he was.

He stopped suddenly, turned to her, and cocked his head. "Didn't you expect to marry? Every woman must."

"Why? Why must every woman marry?"

"Because that is how clans forge friendships. It is how debts are repaid. It is how the world works. Marriage is a duty." He paused and narrowed his eyes. "Or do you not understand duty?"

"I understand duty full well," she answered sharply, "and I have carried out my duties as I have been expected. But I can no longer let duty rule my life."

"Tell me this then. What is ruling your life?"

Mhoire hesitated. She had never considered the question, but the answer leapt to her mind like a dolphin rising from the sea.

"Honor."

"Honor? You call these actions honorable?" His eyes widened in disbelief.

"Aye, I do."

"It is honorable to lie to your father, to mislead our clan, to bring shame on your own clan?"

Mhoire blanched. "I honor myself."

He had no answer to that, but gaped at her for a long moment as if she were a strange animal whose countenance he could not fathom. Then, with a heavy sigh, he took to striding again.

Back and forth he went across the room, his strong arms folded across his chest and his eyes directed at the floor. His brows pulled together in a deep V of concentration, and Mhoire could practically hear his mind working.

After a few moments, he slowed. Turning at the far end of the room, he looked up at her. Rather grimly, she thought, but without rage.

"I will offer you a deal."

"A deal?" She eyed him warily.

"If you can make a living at Dun Darach for one year, I will release you from the marriage agreement, and my clan will find another way to dispense with the Danes."

Mhoire gasped. Hope lifted in her like a bird in flight.

"But . . ." He raised a hand and looked at her keenly. "If you cannot do so, you will marry me willingly and without complaint."

She blinked, scarcely believing her ears. He was offering her a challenge. But he was offering her a chance at freedom, too.

"Your father will agree to this?" she asked with a note of disbelief.

His mouth twisted. "It will take some convincing. But I believe so."

She tensed, suspicious of his intentions. "Why are you doing this?"

He studied her face, running his eyes over her hair, her brow, her mouth, before meeting her gaze.

He replied very evenly. "I am no more eager for marriage than you. But if I must marry, then I prefer it not be to a reluctant bride."

The color rose in her face again, and she cursed herself for the reaction. Terror mixed with joy ran through every bone and muscle. She had no idea of what the future might hold but she knew she must walk toward it.

She had one last question. "How will you know how I fare?"

He lifted one gilded eyebrow. "Because I will go to Dun Darach with you."

Mhoire's mouth fell open. Before she could compose herself enough to close it, he had left.

Striding into the sunlight, Drosten got as far as the outside wall of the hillfort before he realized he had no idea where he was going. But he went through the gate anyway and out toward the fields. It felt good to be moving outside the confines of the fort's walls.

Damnation! Why was he feeling so angry when he had gotten what he wanted? His goal had been to lead the woman into a trap by tempting her with her own desires, and that's exactly what he had done. He had offered her the slimmest chance to take Dun Darach, and she had grabbed it, like a dog snapping at a piece of meat. Drosten knew there was no way she could eke out a living from Dun Darach on her own. Her attempts would come to nothing, and she would have to drop this foolish resistance and marry him. He was sure she would keep her side of the bargain. As Alfred had pointed out, the woman was honest. From now on, all he had to do was bide his time and watch her fail.

And that was the problem.

Drosten stopped, blew out a breath, and scanned the newly planted fields without really seeing them.

He had been trained both to destroy and to protect. For the first time in his life, he found himself wanting to do both to the same person.

Chapter Five

They set off the next day on a journey that was the hardest Mhoire had ever undertaken. With spring coming on, the days were long and growing longer, and Drosten made sure they used every bit of light to travel, rising before the sun and taking only brief breaks to rest the horses and chew on oat cakes until darkness descended. Now, midmorning of the third day, Mhoire found herself wondering if Drosten always drove his men so hard, or if his real intention was to kill her off in the saddle before they even reached Dun Darach. There was no doubt that if a person could die of aching thighs and a sore bottom, she was halfway to the grave.

Her heart, however, sang. She tried not to be too optimistic, tried not to imagine too much. But in the sustained silences that accompanied the long days of riding, her thoughts leapt ahead of her, picturing Dun Darach just over the next ridge, at the bottom of the next glen, suffused in sunlight, waiting.

She knew she was being indulgent. *Don't stir your hopes too much,* she chastised herself. *There is much to accomplish before you can call Dun Darach your own.*

Still, she let herself dream. It was a small, secret pleasure, harmful to no one. And it kept her mind off the mysterious man riding before her.

Drosten sat easily in his saddle, he and his horse as comfortable with each other as only near-constant companions can be. The horse was magnificent, as all Pictish horses were—a pale gray, expertly bred, and fifteen hands high. From this solid perch, Drosten scanned the surroundings, the wind lifting and caressing his fair hair. Clearly these mountains were his domain. Mhoire could see it in the set of his shoulders and the line of his broad back— loose yet alert and, above all, confident.

How Drosten had gotten his father to agree to this deal of theirs, Mhoire could not fathom. They had left Strath Erne with twenty men and nary a hint of opposition. *Odd,* Mhoire mused. These Picts were not very logical. It would certainly have been more expedient to march her to the church. Unless Drosten was so sure of himself—and so scornful of her—that he assumed she would quickly give up her pursuit of independence.

He didn't want to marry, he had said. He had to marry. *But I do not want a reluctant bride.* A shiver ran down Mhoire's spine whenever she recalled those words. What would he expect of her, if it came to marriage? *But it won't,* she quickly assured herself. *I will make Dun Darach prosper if I have to wear the flesh off my bones to do it.*

A fitful sun broke through the clouds, and the wind blew hard. When it gusted under Drosten's short tunic, Mhoire could see the bulge of his leg muscles as he gripped his stallion's flanks. She noticed, too, the blue tattoos etched into his skin—one on his calf and another on his thigh. All the Pictish warriors had them. The skin was pricked with iron pins and herbal dye rubbed into it. Mhoire wondered what this man's images were.

Suddenly, Drosten jerked on his reins, pulled out of line, and slipped his horse tight beside hers.

"What's wrong?"

"What?"

"Your eyes are burning a hole in my back. What's wrong?"

"Nothing."

His stare forced her to look at him.

"You're tired."

"I am not." She gave him a hard stare back.

"You should be."

"You mean after crossing a hundred ridges and fifteen streams, not to mention spending two nights lying on the ground listening to wolves howl their throats dry? You think that would make me tired?"

"Seventeen."

"What?"

"We've crossed seventeen streams. River Ern, River Tay, River Lyon, River Lednock . . ."

"I don't need to know the names."

"You may some day."

She stared straight ahead and pressed her lips together.

"You're tired," he said abruptly. "We'll stop. There's an ash grove just ahead. You can rest out of the wind."

"Nay."

He stiffened in his saddle. She sensed it more than she could see it. His horse sensed it, too, and shook its head, sending its long mane flying. Then, in a flash, Drosten spurred his horse forward. Mhoire frowned as he cantered away and up the next hill through a bank of dark green heather. The man was rude and perhaps a bit impulsive. Mhoire sniffed. She didn't like impulsive men.

She was still frowning a few moments later when Alfred appeared next to her. "Your friend is chasing the wind," she said, pointing her chin toward the crest of the ridge, over which Drosten was fast disappearing.

"Aye," Alfred replied gravely. "Making haste over uncertain ground—bad luck, that."

Within the hour, they came upon yet another water crossing. As the horses padded onto a narrow strip of beach, Mhoire sought out one of the kinder-looking men— a young man named Brian, with dark curly hair and warm brown eyes—to ask where they were. "The Kyles of Bute," he answered. "The narrows. That's the island of Bute over there." He nodded toward the land across the channel.

"An island? Dun Darach is on an island?"

"Aye, down at the tip. Just at the edge of the sea."

She stared southward.

"You can't see it from here, nor the sea neither, because of the angle of the land. But we'll be to Dun Darach soon enough."

"You've been there?"

Brian didn't answer. She tore her gaze from the view and looked at him, but he wouldn't meet her eyes.

"You've been to Dun Darach?" she repeated.

He shifted uneasily in his saddle. "I've been thereabouts."

"And what's it like?"

"Oh, well." He looked everywhere but at her. "It's, ah, well . . ."

"Well?"

Brian cleared his throat. "You'll be there soon. You'll see for yourself." Then he clucked to his horse and moved forward.

Once across the channel, they followed the island's coastline south and rounded its tip. Directly before them was an expanse of short green grass, and in the middle of it stood a large hill. A fairy hill, Mhoire thought it must be, of great bulk and with the curiously rounded top that distinguished all fairy hills. Just beyond it, at the very edge of the island, was an upsurge of rock, flat topped, with steep cliffs on three sides. At its pinnacle was a hillfort, its walls an extension of the ramparts of stone that had been thrust from the earth.

Mhoire's pulse quickened at the sight.

They passed a small lochan, dotted with ducks and rimmed with silky grasses. The sea wind blew against them with a fresh, greening smell. Above Mhoire's head, a stonechat chittered.

She was charmed, almost mesmerized. And so it wasn't until they reached the very base of the hillfort that she realized something was wrong.

The silence was the first peculiar thing Mhoire noticed. She rose in her stirrups and strained her neck to see over the shoulders of the others. Ordinarily, at midday, a hillfort would be filled with the voices of women cooking and washing, of blacksmiths striking iron, of dogs barking and cocks crowing. And there would be men in the fields nearby joking and calling to each other.

She saw no men. No tilled fields.

Her eyes searched out Drosten, who was riding at the front of the line. But this time her stare could not capture his attention.

Anxiety turned into dread. *Where was everyone? Was there a terrible sickness? Had they come to the right place?*

"Wait!" she called out.

The men drew up on their reins and stopped. Drosten turned in his saddle.

She trotted her horse up to his. "This is Dun Darach?"

"Aye."

"I will go first then."

He frowned but nodded.

She moved slowly, examining what was before her with disbelieving eyes. The palisade was gone. On every hillfort, atop the high stone walls, a wooden palisade of tall, pointed timbers was erected. A palisade raised the walls higher and provided added protection. But there was none here. None at all. Moving closer, Mhoire could see why. *Mother of God.* The wall itself was in shambles, half-tumbled to the ground as if a giant creature had come by and swiped it with its paw.

She rode through a yawning break in the wall where a gate must have hung and stopped on the other side. Here was the common ground, where there should have been a kitchen, a stable, a smithy, a butchering room, a tanning shed, an alehouse, and other assorted small buildings, along with the fort's most important structure—the gathering hall. But there were no outbuildings, only chaotic piles of rubble.

The hall was here. Mhoire scanned its outlines. Then her eyes focused on the small fire that was burning in front of the doorway.

It looked so odd, its flames leaping and crackling with life in the midst of stony desolation. There were other signs of life around it: an iron pot hung from a trivet over the flames, and a crude wooden spoon lay nearby. It appeared as if someone had just abandoned her cooking a mere moment ago. Or, perhaps, Mhoire considered with a pang of fear, there were fairy people living here and she just couldn't see them.

She slipped down from her horse. Aye, there was food cooking. She wrinkled her nose. Fish.

Someone was here. Someone—fairy or human—had made this fire and was cooking this meal. Perhaps whoever that was could tell her what, in the name of God and Mary and all the saints, had happened to Dun Darach.

She smoothed her skirt with her hands to wipe off the sweat and stepped to the large wooden door of the gathering hall. Tentatively, she lifted the latch and pushed in. The door squeaked on its hinges as it opened. She stepped over the threshold, and immediately, her eyes were drawn upwards. Where the hall's roof should have been, there was nothing but flat gray sky. And it revealed an interior that was absolutely bare.

Within an hour, Alfred had found the fire's makers, who proved to be entirely human. A small group of women was hiding in a cave carved into the shoreline below, clinging to each other in terror. The rebellious squawk of a goose, which one woman had clasped to her breast, gave their presence away. It required a fair amount of talking on Alfred's part to convince the women that, despite his Pictish accent, he was not the enemy. It took considerably more words before they would accept the idea that there was an Irish princess traveling with him and that she was their kin.

Eventually, however, Alfred persuaded the women to climb back up the cliff. As they assembled before her, Mhoire counted six adult women and one young girl, who looked to be about seven years old. They were a sad sight. All were thin as sparrows and dressed in clothes that had seen much labor. Their hair was limp and their skin sallow. Around each of their necks hung a necklace of sea grapes— the nuts and seeds of seaweed that washed upon the beach from foreign lands and were worn as charms against evil spirits.

The women picked nervously at their skirts. The child, fair-haired and slight, held tightly onto one woman's hand and stared wide-eyed at the big Pictish men and the huge horses with the bronze bridle fittings, which clinked like chimes whenever the animals tossed their heads.

Mhoire took deep breaths. Her head hummed, and her movements seemed nightmarishly slow. But she could not allow herself to give in to her emotions. And she dared not look at Drosten, who waited with his men about ten paces away.

"I am Mhoire ni Colman, from Ardara in the province of Ulster."

The women stirred. "Eveline's child," she heard one whisper to another.

"Aye. I am the daughter of Eveline, whose brother Malcolm was chieftain of this holding. I understand he has passed away. Who has been leader since then?"

The women exchanged puzzled looks.

"The devil, I expect," one called out. She was a middle-aged woman, with a pocked face and a shock of faded brown hair.

"What do you mean?"

"She means no one is leader." The answer came from the woman with the child. She was young, with fine golden hair swept back from an unlined face.

"What is your name?"

"Elanta. And this is my daughter Oran." Elanta stroked the girl's head. Oran leaned against her mother's side.

"What has happened here, Elanta?"

"The Danes came."

"When?"

"Last autumn. We women were on the beach dyeing fleece when the dragonship came up the loch. We ran." She gestured northward. "Up to the chapel. The monks hid us in their cellar. But the fort was set afire. The others . . . killed."

Mhoire laid her hand against her stomach.

"They killed all your men?"

Elanta nodded.

"Your children?"

A muffled sob from someone in the group answered the question.

Mhoire's shoulders slumped. Of all the things she had imagined about Dun Darach, she had never thought of this. "Is there no one else here?"

Elanta shook her head. "Nay. Brigit—" She glanced at the pock-faced woman. "—Brigit was carrying, but the babe was still-born. We are all that is left."

Some of the women wept silently now. Except, Mhoire noticed, the oldest woman, who had a round face and thick gray hair and gazed at her with intense, steady eyes.

"How have you sustained yourselves?"

"We live in the cave below," Elanta replied. "We gather eggs from the cliffs. Seaweed. There's fish in the sea, and silverweed roots, and the woods are full of beechnuts."

Beechnuts. That was famine food.

Mhoire lowered her head. How could this be? As secretive as her mother had been about Dun Darach, to have said nothing of this seemed unbelievable. Her father had told her that her uncle Malcolm had died, but he spoke of it as if it were a recent event, that indeed it was the event that had prompted him to send her here with a husband to take over the holding.

"Why was my mother not told of this tragedy?"

The women lifted their faces in surprise. Elanta's brow wrinkled. "We sent word to your father."

"My father? When?"

"After it happened."

"Last autumn? You sent word last autumn? Please forgive me for my ignorance, but my father never mentioned your troubles." She looked from one woman to the next. "I am so very sorry for what you have endured."

"Your father wasn't," Brigit muttered.

"What do you mean?"

"Your father sent us no aid," Elanta explained, "not even a message of condolence."

"My father—" Mhoire clenched her fists. "I am shamed by my father."

No one replied.

How could he have done this? How could he have abandoned these women when they had no one else to turn to? Had he even told her mother that most of her clan had been murdered?

A thought pierced Mhoire's brain. Had Colman tricked the Picts into thinking they would get a prosperous holding if Drosten married her? Or—*Mother of God*—had the Picts also known that Dun Darach was a wreck?

Her eyes flew to Drosten. His impassive face told her nothing.

"And the king?" she asked Elanta tightly. "Did not the king of Dal Riata help?"

"He has sent us no aid."

Mhoire's fist opened and clenched. A king needed men. In fact, he demanded men: 28 oarsmen from each holding was the rule. And to be sure he got his sailors and other tribute, the king traveled often around his lands.

But he had not come here. For there were no men to be given. Only women. Not worth bothering about. And a fort in ruins.

No wonder Drosten had agreed to let her try to eke a living from Dun Darach. How could she possibly succeed?

Her anger gave her strength. Calmly, she asked each of the women to introduce herself and describe her lineage. By the time the explanations were finished, the women seemed friendlier and less fearful.

They were also casting curious looks at the Picts, who were still standing quietly to one side, holding their horses' bridles or leaning against the beasts' flanks.

Mhoire cleared her throat. "You are, no doubt, wondering why these men are here."

"Why are *you* here?" Elanta asked.

"Me?"

The women looked at her expectantly. Obviously, her father had not bothered to alert them to her coming.

"Well, I'm here to . . . be your chieftain."

The women traded baffled looks. Mhoire winced. She knew how strange her statement must sound. Neither in Ireland nor in Dal Riata was a woman ever chieftain.

Grainne spoke up. "What I think Mhoire means to say is that since Colman did not send help to you, she, as Eveline's only child, has come to do what she can. Isn't that right, Mhoire?"

Mhoire thought that was near enough to the truth to not be called a lie. Her mouth curved in a small, false smile.

"And why are the Picts here and not your father's warriors?" Elanta ran her eyes thoughtfully over the band of men.

"Ah. The Picts. Well, their leader, Drosten . . ." He nodded once to identify himself. His eyes were riveted on her. ". . . He and I have an understanding. A kind of bargain."

The women turned back to her, their eyes bright with curiosity.

"My father wants me to marry Drosten."

A few eyebrows went up.

"But I don't wish to marry him."

The eyebrows went down.

"Or anyone," she hastened to add.

Mouths dropped open. Saying she didn't want to marry was about as absurd a statement as saying she was their chieftain.

Mhoire plunged on. "The agreement that Drosten and I have is that if I—with all of you—manage to survive here for a year, he and his men will return to their homeland." She waved her hand vaguely eastward. "If we can't, then, well, then he and I will marry." She finished limply.

The women looked at each other and then peered over at the men. Whispered conversation ensued.

Mhoire frowned. "I know you must hate having the Picts here, given the fact that their forebears have battled with yours. But I promise you I will do my best to get them to leave."

"We'll keep any man who knows how to plow," Brigit called out. Some of the others giggled. Oran, Mhoire noticed, was staring round-eyed at Drosten, who soberly winked at her. The little girl shyly smiled back, and buried herself farther into her mother's skirts.

Mhoire shifted on her feet in irritation and affected what she hoped was a quelling scowl.

"I'm certain we can manage the plowing and every other task that needs to be done. I have only a little food with me, but I do have a fair amount of seed." She got the women's attention with that—it was the chieftain's duty to provide seed. "Everything is in my saddle bags, and once we unload them, we can sort it all out and make plans."

She strode toward the horses. The men had distributed her baggage among them. "Grainne," she called, "would you help me, please?"

As she and Grainne approached the horses, she heard Drosten say something quietly in a language she didn't understand. The men turned to their steeds and began to remove her bags.

"Nay," she snapped. "We can do this ourselves."

The men looked at Drosten. He crossed his arms over his broad chest. "Some of these bags are as heavy as a cow. Do you really want to break your back hauling them around?"

Mhoire walked up to him, a spot of color staining each cheek. "I am quite capable of carrying my own baggage." She brought her hands to her hips. He was so tall that she had to bend her head back to look in his eyes. Which, she noticed with a shock, were a brilliant, piercing blue. "Besides," she hissed, "I can't see why you want to help me, given that it's completely in your interest to have me fail."

Drosten put his hands on his hips, mimicking her posture, and brought his face down to hers. "I don't think having a few strong men take your bags down from their horses is going to make a difference in whether you succeed or fail, do you?"

She dropped her eyes to his hard jaw. "Dun Darach is my home and I will give the orders. And when the time comes to evaluate how I have fared here, I do not want any questions about whether or not my accomplishments are my own."

She chanced another look into his eyes. They were darker now, the pupils wider and more clouded.

A few long seconds passed. Then a muscle tightened in Drosten's cheek. He straightened. "As you wish. The unpacking is yours."

He turned to his horse. "Besides, we're going hunting. You have nine mouths to feed. I have twenty." He tore his spear from its holster. "Come with me," he called to his men. And he stalked off down the hill.

Mhoire frowned at his back and then glanced toward the women. All eyes were fastened on her.

"Pay him no mind," she insisted.

The women smiled.

Chapter Six

A few hours later, Drosten and his men returned to the fort dragging the carcasses of two red deer. They gutted and skinned the animals and dug a large hole outside the gathering hall. There they buried the meat amid hot stones, and, while it cooked, went to work on the remains. Bones would be used for spearheads, matlocks, needles, tooth picks, and toggles; sinew for cordage; fat for lamp oil; stomachs, bladders, and large intestines as bags for carrying water.

Ordinarily, Drosten would have mingled with the group, but tonight a curious mood had overtaken him. He carried one of the deer hides to the other side of the courtyard, where he could be alone. Pulling out his dagger, he began scraping the flesh from the skin so it could be tanned. It was messy work, and one of his men could easily have done it. But Drosten couldn't bear to be idle, especially when he had so much on his mind.

The Irishwoman was unusual, that was for sure. He was used to sizing up men—his life depended on it—and he had watched Mhoire that day with a critical eye. He had found nothing to criticize. She bore the weight of what must have been devastating news on her small, sturdy shoulders with barely a flinch. Though her eyes revealed her distress, she remained calm and gracious—except, of course, when she was seething at him. But that aside, the woman showed remarkable control, more than many men would in the same circumstances. How had she learned to contain her emotions so well? And why?

And *damnation,* she was beautiful. He hadn't been able to take his eyes off her. *That* was annoying. He had better things to do than stare at a woman. But, Lord above, what a pleasure it was to look at that cloud of dark hair, those dove-gray eyes, that slender body with its tiny waist. Drosten let out a heavy sigh. He had learned early on in their journey to Dun Darach never to ride behind her. What would his men think if their leader fell off his horse because he was too busy gawking at a woman to keep his eye on the rock-strewn turf?

But nighttime was different. Then, as Mhoire slept curled up like a puppy a few yards away, he could stare as much as he liked. *But this puppy has teeth,* he muttered to himself, *don't forget that.* She snapped at him in a way his men would never dare to. Drosten shook his head. Wouldn't he like to kiss that stubborn mouth of hers until it grew soft under his.

"Drosten!"

"What?" He scowled and looked up, the bloody hide in his hands.

Alfred strode toward him. "Are you thinking we'll camp up here, then?"

"Aye. It's the best vantage point." Drosten wiped his knife on the hem of his tunic. "We'll want to keep a watch posted all night, in case we get unexpected visitors."

"What about the women? They've made their hiding hole in that godforsaken cave."

"We'll let them stay there tonight. Tomorrow we'll put a roof on this place and bring them up here."

Alfred gave Drosten a skeptical look. "You think the Irishwoman will let you order them about?"

"Nay." Drosten rummaged around in his pack and pulled out a whetstone. "I think the Irishwoman would throw herself over a cliff before she'd let me tell her what to do. But I'll wager that after spending one night in that cold, wet cave, she'll think that moving into a newly thatched gathering hall is the best idea she's ever come up with."

"Is this another one of your strategies? Get her to think it's her idea to sleep in the hall?"

"It is."

"Hmmph."

For a few moments, Alfred watched Drosten's hands as he ran his knife across the whetstone. The Pictish leader seemed unusually intent on the job, drawing the knife across the stone slightly more forcefully than was necessary.

"That companion of hers is a devil-woman, if you ask me," Alfred finally announced. "Just a little while ago, I asked her for a pot to cook in. Just a simple pot to boil the deer livers in, mind you, and she near killed me with her questions. 'What do you want it for?' she asked. 'And how long do you intend to keep it?' 'And why didn't you bring your own?' You'd think the thing was made of gold." Alfred shook his head. "Irishwomen! A plague on them, I say."

There was no reply.

Alfred cast his gaze over the half-tumbled wall. "It's a woeful sight, this. Your father surprised me—consenting to this alliance with Colman. He's bending his pride, he is."

"He's doing what has to be done."

"The Irish lass didn't know about the burning, did she?"

"Obviously not."

"She'll never get this place to thrive on her own. But you knew that all along, didn't you?"

Drosten said nothing and kept working the knife against the stone.

"It's women like her who drive me to the brink," Alfred continued. "Got too many notions in them. Makes them unpredictable. Steady and true, that's what I like."

Drosten didn't answer.

"Do you think she wants to be a nun?"

"She's no nun."

"How do you know?"

"I know."

"Hmm. Maybe she's a witch, then."

"Alfred. Don't be daft."

"Well, it's witches who live alone."

Drosten ran his thumb along the blade again.

"Maybe she's running from another man."

Drosten started and pricked his skin. Another man? A bead of blood bubbled up. He sucked on his thumb. What other man?

"Uh, oh," Alfred muttered. "Here comes trouble herself."

Drosten looked up, his thumb in his mouth. Mhoire was marching toward them, her lips set, a flush high on her cheekbones. His heart began to thud in his chest.

She stopped a few feet from him. "May I speak with you alone, please?"

Drosten opened his mouth and turned to Alfred, but his friend had drifted away.

He held up his hands, one holding the knife and the other the whetstone. "Here I am." He smiled, but Mhoire didn't notice.

"You tricked me."

Drosten's gut went cold. "I did not."

Her eyes were as gray as smoke, but he could see the fire smoldering within them. He could happily burn in it, he realized.

"You knew Dun Darach had been destroyed."

"Aye. Do you think my clan would have agreed to our union without evaluating what we would get from it?"

"Why didn't you tell me? You heard me talk about Dun Darach with hope in my heart. You must have suspected I was ignorant of this."

Drosten tossed the whetstone on his pack. Then he slipped the dagger into the sheath on his belt. "I suspected, aye."

"And you said nothing." She searched out his eyes until they met hers. "You said nothing. And you made this . . . this deal, knowing what impossible odds I would face here." She drew a shaky breath. Tears welled in her eyes. "That, sir, was not fair."

Drosten raised both eyebrows. "Not fair? Let me tell you this. If you want to act like a man, you must do battle like a man. I need Dun Darach, not for myself but for the welfare of my country, and I will do what I must to get it. And don't think you can melt my heart with tears because you won't."

Mhoire averted her gaze and blinked rapidly. "These are not tears! You will *never* see me cry!"

They stood silently. Neither looked at the other.

After a few moments, Drosten ran his hand through his hair and stole a glance at Mhoire. Her body was as rigid as a broomstick, except for her hair, which had loosened in long, curling tendrils around her face. He couldn't see the expression in her eyes, which were cast in the direction of the sea. Only the profile of her long, dark lashes.

"You would have accepted the bargain anyway."

She drew a deep breath. He watched her breast rise and fall. "Aye, I would have. Still, you must have enjoyed hearing my foolish dreams and watching them get blown to bits."

He studied her a moment. She seemed thoroughly sickened by him. His own anger ebbed and despondency returned. Ordinarily, another person's opinion of him had about as much weight as the shavings off his knife. But he hated the fact that Mhoire believed him to be so foul.

"I would have you know that I never revel in another person's sorrow. Never."

She raised cold eyes to his. "Then pray tell me why you torment us with this meat."

"Torment you?" His brows drew together. "What are you talking about?"

"You know how hungry these women are. We can smell this venison cooking even from the cave."

"Everyone is welcome to partake of it. There is plenty."

"I see." Mhoire nodded stiffly. "Of course it is in your interest to win the favor of the women."

Drosten flushed. He opened his mouth to reply but closed it when he noticed Oran scampering toward them.

"Mhoire!" She came to a breathless halt beside them. "Supper is ready!"

Mhoire leaned down, laid her hand on the girl's fair head, and smiled. Drosten's heart skipped a beat.

"Thank you, Oran," Mhoire said. "I'll come now."

The child slipped her hand into Mhoire's and turned to Drosten. "Did you fell the deer, Drosten?"

"One of them, aye."

Excitement lit her eyes. "We killed a deer once. It was in the winter and there was much snow on the ground. The deer was limping, and it couldn't run in the snow. So we circled it. We didn't have a spear so we smashed its head with a stone." Suddenly serious, Oran's voice lowered. "My grandmother said that was not a bad thing. She said God had sent us the deer because we were so hungry and we must take it any way we could."

Drosten dropped to his haunches before her and rested his arms on his knees. "Your grandmother was right, little one. And if the deer was injured, it was a mercy to kill it."

Oran stared at him soberly and then she brightened. "It was very tasty. We ate every bit." Her eyes widened. "Your deer smells as good as our deer did."

Drosten dared not respond to that.

"Mhoire brought us apples so we're having those for supper."

Rising, he glanced at Mhoire, who was looking at the child and biting her lip. "That sounds very good as well," he said.

"Would you like to eat with us and have some? You could tell us how you killed the deer."

"Thank you, little one," Drosten answered gently. "But I should stay up here with the men."

"Oh." Oran's face fell.

Drosten risked another look at Mhoire. This time she met his eyes with a strained expression and gave a tiny nod.

Drosten squatted before Oran again. "Perhaps you would like some of this venison to go along with your apples?"

Oran's eyes widened even more. "Oh, aye! I would like that very much." She stole a look at Mhoire before adding shyly, "Would there be enough for my mother, and for Mhoire, and the others, too?"

"There is plenty enough for us all," Drosten responded, rising. "Run along now, and as soon as it's cooked, one of the men will bring some down to the cave."

Oran smiled broadly and looked up at Mhoire, tugging on her hand. "Can we go back now? I want to tell the others."

Mhoire gave Oran a half-smile in return. Then she met Drosten's eyes and held them with a look that set his heart once again a-thudding.

They walked away hand in hand, the child babbling, the woman leaning toward her in response. Mhoire's parting expression had been inscrutable, but for once Drosten hadn't detected any anger in it. It was a small thing, but he cradled the memory against his chest as he would a tiny, fragile animal.

Mhoire did not sleep much that night. The cave was so cold it made her teeth chatter, the ground oozed with mud, and frigid water dripped from the ceiling. Although she wrapped her wool mantle tightly about her, it could not keep away the chill nor the demons that swirled in the black night air.

She rose at first light with her thoughts gnawing at her conscience the way a rat gnaws on bone. What right had she to try to make her own way? To reject a marriage that would help others? To put her desires above their needs? She was doing something terribly wrong, asking for something she shouldn't be asking for, causing too much trouble. But, merciful God, when she thought of a future like her mother's, it seemed as black as any cave and just as frightening.

She carried out the morning's activities numbly. It was

Grainne who got the women organized. They looked over the fields together and decided which plots of land would be the best to plant with the seed Mhoire had brought. The moon was waxing, which meant it was a good time for sowing, and everyone was eager to begin.

By the time they had made their plans, the day was half over, and the women dispersed to tackle the necessary chores. Grainne had her own plan. At first light she had noticed that the men were felling timber and gathering bentgrass, and she had pestered Alfred until he confessed that Drosten was intent on thatching the roof of the gathering hall before the day was done.

"If there's going to be a roof on your hall, then you have a right to sleep under it," she asserted to Mhoire, after the women had left them alone in the fields below the fort.

"I suppose so," Mhoire answered absently. She was gazing at a grove of trees to the north, set like a dark green jewel in the grassy countryside.

"I'm going to find Drosten and tell him that we're moving our things out of that horrid cave and into the hall, and we don't care what he thinks of it." She noticed Mhoire's preoccupation. "Why don't you go for a walk to that grove? It will do you good to move about."

"I keep wondering if those are oak trees," Mhoire mused. "Dun Darach—'Fort of the Oaks,' remember?"

"You go on. Don't worry about us." She tapped a long, bony finger on Mhoire's chest. "We don't need *any* men."

Mhoire gave her another slight smile and then slowly walked off.

Rather than plunge across the overgrown fields, she headed for the beach. The sand was damp there, and her soft leather boots sunk into it only a little. Still, the weight of her worries hung heavy on her shoulders.

Rock pipits hopped among the rocks in the water close to shore as she trudged along. A little farther off, the sleek, dark heads of seals bobbed in the swells.

After half a mile, she left the beach and struck inland, cutting across the weedy fields and pastures to the grove, which was tucked into a great green hollow. A flat-topped stone wall enclosed the entrance.

Mhoire went through the gate and found herself amongst not oaks, but cherry trees. A cluster here. A cluster there. Upright, slender, and graceful. In the center of the hollow stood a small stone building. As Mhoire approached, she noticed the roof was missing, and the interior lay empty. Nila, the older woman who had watched her so steadily the day before, sat on a bench against the outer wall.

Mhoire lowered herself beside her. "What is this place?" she asked softly.

"St. Blane's Chapel."

They faced the low side of the hollow. Directly before them, a little distance beyond the stone wall, rose the large, hummocky hill Mhoire had noticed when she had first approached the hillfort.

"The fairy hill," she said, nodding toward it.

Nila smiled. "The monks named it *Suidhe Bhlain*—St. Blane's Hill—after they arrived many generations ago. But, aye, it's a fairy hill."

Mhoire glanced at her. Although Nila was Elanta's mother, in some ways the two were very different. Elanta was fair and thin as thread; Nila was stocky, almost square-shaped, with iron-gray hair. Elanta carried an air of earthy femininity; Nila seemed veiled in mystery.

"Is this where you hid from the Danes?" Mhoire asked.

"Aye. There is a root cellar behind us in the cliff. The Danes burned the chapel, as you can see. And they killed all the monks."

"Killed the monks? My God!"

"The Danes are pagan, child. They wanted the gold chalices and the silver crosses. The monks would not easily give them up."

They talked for a while. Dun Darach had been a crossroads, Nila explained, with ships constantly sailing past. Tradesmen had brought coriander and dill from France; nuts, dates, and sweetmeats from the Mediterranean. In turn, Dun Darach and the other surrounding holdings had exported leather, eider down, and furs.

"The destruction of the hillfort and the chapel was a grievous blow," Mhoire noted.

Nila nodded gravely.

"Why didn't you leave Dun Darach? Once everything was gone?"

Nila met her eyes. "Because sometimes you must choose your ground and stay on it."

Mhoire considered Nila's statement. "Well, I'm beginning to think that the best thing I could do is run up that hill and let the fairies take me away."

"Why did you come here?"

Mhoire scanned the view before her—the sturdy hill, the grassy fields, the blue plate of the sea beyond them. "I thought if I journeyed to a new place, everything would be different. I wanted a place that had . . . life."

She looked down at her lap. A familiar emptiness fell over her like mist. In her father's holding, she had had no friend but Grainne. The dark fort had welcomed few visitors. It had sheltered only pain. And secrets.

"But I have been very selfish," she went on. "I see now that there are more important concerns than my own. You, the other women, the child, you are all starving. I cannot ignore that."

"Nay, you cannot ignore that," Nila conceded. "You made a choice to come here. And with choice comes responsibility. Besides, child, you can't drop into life like an angel from the sky. You must create it."

Mhoire closed her eyes.

"What about the man?" Nila asked.

Mhoire's eyes flew open. "What about him?"

"What do you think of him?"

"I . . . he . . . I don't know what to think of him." She sensed Nila looking at her but avoided her gaze. "He confuses me."

"As you confuse him, no doubt." Mhoire could hear the smile in Nila's voice. "Do you want to marry him?"

Mhoire shook her head. "Nay. But he has every right to demand it." Mhoire twisted her hands in her lap. "It would be better for the others if I married him."

"It would be easier for the others if you married him. But better? It is too early to tell."

Mhoire asked the question that had been haunting her. "Why did my mother leave Dun Darach?"

Nila looked toward the sea, toward the past. "Your mother did not have a choice."

"Colman was a horrible husband."

"Aye. But you must remember, child—" Nila's voice sounded sad but deliberate. "—your mother made a promise to him. And she accepted what came of it."

A promise. A living death.

"What was my mother like when she was young?"

Nila reached out and laid her hand over Mhoire's. "She was like you. Very brave."

Mhoire shook her head. "I don't think of myself—nor my mother—as brave."

"Your mother was braver than you know. But she changed after she married."

Tears welled in Mhoire's eyes. She blinked them away. "You miss her."

Mhoire nodded and wiped her eyes with her sleeve. "I wish . . ." Her throat closed up. She tried again. "I wish she had spoken with me more. Like a mother." An image rose in Mhoire's mind—Eveline sitting in her chamber on a cold day, shoulders slumped, staring silently out the window.

Nila's voice was as light as a feather in the wind. "Sometimes when we carry a great sorrow, we can see no one's burden but our own."

Tears spilled down Mhoire's face. Her right hand closed around the leather pouch that rested against her breast.

"You are carrying a charm?" Nila asked.

Mhoire sniffled hard. She looked down at the pouch. "Pebbles. I found them after my mother died. Three round pebbles in a silver box." She looked at Nila then, her eyes swollen with tears. "Do you think I should marry him?"

"I think you must follow your own path."

"But I'm so afraid," Mhoire whispered.

Kindness pooled in the old woman's eyes. She took Mhoire's hand and gripped it hard.

For a few minutes, they sat in silence. Then Mhoire roused herself. "I must go back. It's getting late."

"Aye. Go back along the beach. That's the best way."

Mhoire rose and looked down at the old woman. "Won't you walk with me?"

Nila waved her away. "You go along, child. I'll return shortly."

A half-hour later, Mhoire stepped onto the beach. Clouds were scudding across the open sky. The tide was up, almost high. To avoid the cold surf, Mhoire picked her way across the cobblestones that littered the upper reaches, between the sand and the grassy bank.

She had to watch her footing carefully so as not to turn an ankle or slip on seaweed. Absorbed in that task, it was a few moments before she noticed the stones under her boots. They were all colors: white, pink, green with red flecks, dark blue striated with thin bands of black. She dropped to her knees. Carefully, she picked up one and then another, turning each stone in her hand and looking at it closely. Then she pulled the leather pouch from around her neck and emptied its contents into her palm.

Her stones—her mother's stones—were the same as these that lay all about her. The same shades of pink and green and blue. Beautifully smooth and rounded by the sea. They were Dun Darach's stones, and her mother had treasured them all these years.

A deep sob hurled up from Mhoire's chest. Then another and another. Her lungs compressed in a great spasm and then released in a flood of tears. She gulped for breath, and her body convulsed again. She wept uncontrollably, helplessly. It was as if her soul, suppressed for so long, had finally seized her body. And it poured out dark streams of sorrow.

She could not say how long she crouched there. But

eventually the sobs lessened and she felt the hard stones digging into her knees. She wiped her face with her sleeve. Clumsily she tucked her three pebbles back into their pouch and slipped the leather strap over her neck. She pushed herself to her feet. The sky now was calm, and clouds lay across it in long silver ribbons. The sea was the color of pewter and just as smooth. Where light filtered through a cloud and beamed upon the water, it shimmered palely, like an angel's wing.

Mhoire blinked back the last of her tears, tucked her hair behind her ears, and straightened her shoulders. Dun Darach was directly in front of her. She strode toward it.

Chapter Seven

"**I** suppose we could use our daggers." Mhoire sat back on her heels in a corner of the gathering hall, her brow furrowed. "But I wish we had more of them. We must dig those weeds out of the fields with something."

"I know where we can get more." Grainne gestured to the other side of the hall where the men's belongings were piled. "Those men have daggers and knives of all descriptions hanging from them."

The women had spent the night at one end of the gathering hall; the warriors had slept at the other end—except for the sentries whom Drosten had posted to keep watch, and Drosten himself, who had slept outside.

"Grainne! We're not going to steal their daggers."

Grainne's face set in stubborn lines.

Mhoire turned back to her own neat pile of possessions. She wished she had brought more things with her.

Suddenly, Oran's high voice rung out. "You have to wash your hands!"

Mhoire turned on her knees and faced the center of the hall. Four of Drosten's men were standing in front of the hearth fire on which Elanta was cooking porridge in an iron pot. Tiny Oran was flitting from one man to another, prying their brawny hands from the metal cups they were holding and inspecting them closely.

"Nay, nay," she was saying to one scruffy individual, shaking her head. "Your hands are too dirty. You must

58

wash them before you can eat." She pushed him in the direction of the wash bucket.

Mhoire rose to her feet. "What's this?"

Elanta paused in her stirring, looked at Mhoire out of the corner of her eye, and then continued with her task. "Breakfast, of course." She filled one man's cup and gave him a brilliant smile. He blushed, mumbled a word of thanks, and settled cross-legged on the ground.

Mhoire walked up to the fire. "I thought I explained this, Elanta. The men take care of themselves, and we take care of ourselves." Two red spots formed on Mhoire's cheeks. Elanta's face, on the other hand, was as placid as a summer's day.

"Good!" Oran's voice piped up. Brian, the curly-haired young man, walked up to the porridge pot, grinning.

Elanta colored slightly. "We thought it only fair, Mhoire," Elanta explained as she filled his bowl, "that we share our porridge with the men since they had shared their venison with us." Elanta filled another bowl and held it out to Mhoire. "Besides, they are our guests."

Mhoire sighed and took the bowl. "Not exactly." She picked up a spoon and ate silently.

Elanta settled Oran next to her, and Mhoire dropped down beside them. She noticed the resemblance between mother and daughter, especially in their sheaths of silky blond hair. She couldn't help but feel a pang of jealousy over Elanta's magnetic beauty.

"The Picts are your enemy, are they not? They have overrun this country numerous times in the past."

"Och. That was a long time ago." She glanced at the men and then at Mhoire. "Anyway, they look peaceful enough now, don't they?"

They certainly did. Mhoire frowned as she watched the big warriors contentedly shovel food in their mouths. They were an ill-kempt bunch, in their stained tunics and scuffed boots. But they looked quite tame. Indeed, all of their attention seemed to be devoted to two benign tasks: getting food in their stomachs and stealing surreptitious glances at Elanta.

"And where's your leader then this morning?" Brigit called over to the men. "Or is he such a tough one he doesn't need to eat?"

"Drosten, you mean? Oh, he loves his food as well as any of us. But you won't find him cleaning himself up for breakfast because a woman says so." His mouth split in a good-natured grin.

"Aye, that's for sure." A bear of a man with a red beard glanced around at his colleagues and gestured with his spoon. "That's how he lost his last wife, remember?"

Mhoire stilled. His last wife?

"Fionna," Brian stated. The men all nodded.

"Who's Fionna?" Elanta asked.

Brian leaned forward conspiratorially. "A beautiful princess." The rest of the men nodded again. "The daughter of Domangart mac Bili. She and Drosten were betrothed to marry. He would have been king of the province if he had married her."

"What happened?" Elanta's attention was riveted on Brian. Even Brigit had her ears cocked. Mhoire kept her eyes lowered on her empty bowl.

"Ah. It was quite a scandal—" Brian looked around and lowered his voice. "Drosten was daft for her."

Daft for her? Mhoire felt a sinking sensation in her stomach. Against her will, she leaned slightly forward.

The red-bearded man spoke with his mouth full: "She had yellow hair."

"Aye," Brian added. There was a dreamy look in his eyes. "A tall woman. Huge purple eyes and—" He colored and cleared his throat. "Well, like I said, Drosten was daft for her. But he had responsibilities, you see. The Britons were raising hell along the border, and we was out chasing them constantly."

Suddenly, the red-bearded man reached out and clapped Brian on the shoulder. "That's when you sliced off your first head, lad. Remember that, do you, eh?"

Color crept up Brian's neck. "I do that, aye, Fergus." He managed to look embarrassed and smug at the same time.

"Only sixteen, he was." Fergus's grin showed a row of teeth as tangled as his hair and beard. "We knew he'd be a grand fighter. Sliced it clean like he was taking the top off a radish."

"So tell us about the princess, lad," Brigit demanded. "Enough about you."

"Oh, aye, well—" Brian looked around again. Clearly, this was gossip. "Fionna rejected Drosten. Chose another man."

The women cast astonished looks at each other. Pictish princesses clearly had more autonomy than most Irish or Scottish females.

"It was shortly before the wedding," Brian continued, "and Drosten and all of us had ridden right to her father's fort from one of the worst battles we had been in." The men nodded, remembering. "Drosten had this gash in his head where a Briton had gotten him with an axe. We couldn't believe he could even stay on his horse, but he had promised Fionna he'd be there, so be there we had to be. Well, we got to her father's fort, and we was all eating in the hall." Brian lowered his voice even more. Everyone inched closer. "Right in the middle of supper, she announced it to Drosten, just like that. Told him she was marrying Uurgust. 'Drosten,' she said, 'you're uncivilized. I can't marry you.' Everyone heard it."

"That's horrible," Elanta whispered.

"Aye. Twas." Brian shook his head. "Drosten, he just stood up and walked away. Didn't say a word. Pale as a ghost, he was. Then we all got back on our horses and rode home."

"He's never been the same since," Fergus said mournfully. "Not near as much fun in him."

"Won't have nothing to do with women, either," Brian said, lifting his brows. "The fathers, they all want him to marry their daughters. His mother was the daughter of a king, you see, so he's in the royal line. Quite eligible, you might say. But Drosten, he won't as much look at a woman twice."

"Women! Bah!" Fergus spit out. "Here's a man who's had no mother since he was a wee thing. How could he not be a little rough around the edges? You'd think a woman would expect that, wouldn't you?" He looked around at his companions for confirmation. Their heads bobbed.

"What happened to his mother?" The words slipped out of Mhoire's mouth before she could stop them.

The men grew silent. Brian looked down at his hands and fidgeted.

"Did she die?" she persisted.

"He doesna like us to talk about it." The other men shifted in their positions. Fergus scratched his head.

Elanta bent toward Brian. "Please tell us what happened."

Brian fumbled with his spoon. "I canna. It's not a thing to be spoken of. Has to do with the Danes, you see. Drosten's mother was killed, and his sister stolen away."

Mhoire stared at Brian, stunned.

"Did they find her?" Elanta asked.

"The sister? Nay. Never. Gormach went to Daneland many times, looking. Drosten did, too, when he was older. They hired spies." Brian shook his head sadly. "Never found her."

" 'Twas a tragedy, that's for sure." Fergus shook his head. His face crumpled like old linen. "My family—myself, my father, my mother, my brothers—we was all in the hills with the cattle that summer. That's how we missed it." He sighed. "Drosten's mother, she was a good woman. Kind to everyone. Never a harsh word from her. Smart as a druid. She was the one that ran the holding, truth be told."

"How old was he when this happened?" Elanta asked.

"Drosten?" Brian looked at Fergus. "Nine years, perhaps?"

"More like seven," Fergus corrected glumly. "At most. Just a wee thing he was. Still gives him nightmares. Tis why he sleeps by himself. Outside. Doesna want to wake us."

They all quieted, contemplating the horror of Fergus's words. Mhoire understood the agony of a mother dying. *And his sister gone, too.*

"Why do you say Drosten never forgave himself?" Brigit asked. "The poor lad. He was only a child. What could he have done to fight off the Danes?"

Brian looked at Fergus and raised his eyebrows in a silent question. Fergus tightened his lips and shook his head.

Suddenly, a voice boomed from the doorway. "What are you doing in here?"

Every head bent upward.

Chapter Eight

Drosten loomed on the threshold, brows lowered, his head almost scraping the lintel. But for an instant Mhoire saw past his intimidating figure. She imagined the boy behind the man, as tender as new-grown grass, and wondered how much pain still writhed within him.

"What is going on here?" He growled a command, but Mhoire didn't understand it. His men did, and they scrambled to their feet. Drosten pointed to the door, and they sheepishly filed out.

"Do you know what he's saying?" Mhoire whispered to Elanta.

"I don't know. It must be the old Pictish language. It's what the Picts spoke before the monks came and taught them Gaelic."

Mhoire rose and eyed Drosten warily. He had stopped speaking and was frowning at the doorway through which the men had disappeared. "There is no need to shout, Drosten. Your men have done nothing wrong. I'll have no raised voices in this hall."

He turned. His blues eyes flared.

"First of all, I am not shouting. Secondly, I have men out in that courtyard who have been up all night guarding this fort and they need to be relieved. We're in a dangerous situation, and I won't have soldiers lolling over their porridge bowls."

Mhoire's chin went up. Damn the man! He may have

suffered losses, but he had certainly covered them up with a thick, insolent attitude. "No one asked you to stand a guard."

"Do you want to be killed in your sleep?" His voice held a cutting tone she had never heard in it before.

"Nay, I don't fancy dying in the night. A guard is useful. But it's not us you're guarding. It's yourselves. The fort wouldn't require a guard if there weren't so many large male creatures in it to attract attention. These women, remember, have managed to live here quietly and without incident for a long time."

"Well, we're here now. And I don't want your women distracting my men from their duties."

"Distracting! They're the ones lingering about and telling stories and keeping people from doing their work."

"And—" one golden brow lifted—"what were you doing?"

"I? Nothing! Elanta offered your men porridge, and they took it. I did not wish her to make the offer."

"Then it appears you need to exercise more control over your women."

"As you do over your men?"

Drosten's head snapped back. "I will instruct my men to stay away from your women, and they will obey me." His eyes began to burn like a kindling fire, and she felt a flash of satisfaction.

"You want to make this fort prosper by yourself—fine," he continued. "You say you don't want any help. Fine. We won't give you any. But I won't risk getting my head cut off, and I will do what I think I have to do to keep this fort safe."

"Fine. Do what you have to do. Just remember we don't need your help."

Drosten's hard jaw tensed. He nodded.

Mhoire nodded.

Elanta cleared her throat. "Er, Mhoire. We could use a little help with food."

Mhoire whipped around to face her. "We'll hunt our own food."

Elanta flushed and bowed her head.

Mhoire turned back to Drosten. "It's settled then."

Drosten made for the door.

"Wait!" Oran chirped. "I have an idea!"

Heads swiveled to look at the little girl sitting on the floor.

"Listen," Oran continued, jumping to her feet. "This is my idea." She hopped from one foot to the other, like a little bird. "Whatever Drosten fells, we cook. And whatever we fell, he cooks. And everybody gets to eat everything!" She lifted her hands, palms up, as if to show how simple a scheme it was.

Mhoire frowned. It was not such a bad arrangement. If they did what Oran was suggesting, both sides would be making an equal contribution to the welfare of the group. They all had to eat. And she was fully confident of her bow-hunting skills. She looked over at Drosten.

He shrugged. "I'll do it if you will. I wouldn't mind the taste of a woman's cooking for a change."

Mhoire arched an eyebrow. "A woman's cooking? You think you'll be the one to get all the game?"

Drosten blinked. Then he grasped her meaning. "And you think you will?"

"I think you may find yourself doing considerably more cooking than you anticipate."

Drosten looked incredulous.

She was provoking him. Odd, but that left her a little breathless.

An anticipatory hum coursed through the air.

Elanta cleared her throat again. "So, it's settled then?"

Drosten and Mhoire locked eyes and nodded as one.

Brigit and Elanta exchanged a knowing look.

Oran peered at Drosten, and then Mhoire, and then Drosten again, uncertain of what was going on or what should happen next. "Drosten," she finally chirruped. "Do you want the rest of my porridge? You can have it if you wash your hands."

Drosten threw back his head and laughed—a deep, warm laugh that Mhoire realized she had never heard from him before. Something in her belly fluttered.

He regarded his hands, one side and then the other, spreading wide his large fingers. "Little one, it would take half a day to wash these hands properly." He looked up and smiled at the girl, whose innocent words seemed to have expelled whatever it was that had been troubling him. "You finish your porridge. I have some serious hunting to do."

A few hours later, Mhoire was kneeling in the overgrown field, a burlap sack full of seed open before her. She plunged both of her hands into the sack and let the small, wispy ovules run through her fingers. The seed was still dry. Good. She had brought two sacks each of barley and oat seed, and they were going to need all of it. With oats and barley, the women could make bread and porridge. She could hunt game, and they could forage for wild greens and berries. That would be enough to live on. But if this crop failed—well, Mhoire dared not think about it. Everyone knew that when the oats withered, entire clans of emaciated people clasped hands and threw themselves over a cliff into the sea rather than face the slow torture of death by starvation.

Today they would start planting. A good day, Mhoire thought, as she straightened and looked around. The sun was out and the larks were singing. Most of the women, along with little Oran, were on their knees digging out weeds. Elanta was scraping the ground with a rake that had escaped the fort's burning. Grainne furrowed the soil with deer antlers, which she had pried away from Alfred after considerable harassment.

Mhoire walked over to where the others were working, dropped to her knees, and laid her bow on the ground beside her. She shifted the quiver on her back into a more comfortable position. All the talk about the Danes had made her anxious for their safety, and she had decided this morning to always carry her weapons with her.

She slipped her dagger from the leather sheath tied to her calf, grasped an offending weed with her left hand, and thrust the blade into the ground. This was going to be tedious work.

"Put some rhubarb on your hair, Brigit. Twill bring the color out." That was Elanta speaking.

"Do you think so, then?"

"Aye. Twould brighten it. Make it a bit more eye-catching."

"Eye-catching is it you want to be?" Grainne paused in her raking to ask. "And whose eye is it that you want to catch?"

Brigit sat back on her heels and pushed a lock of muddy brown hair back from her sweaty forehead. "I think I rather fancy that red-bearded one. He's got a look about him."

"Aye, the look of an ox," Grainne snorted.

"Mayhap. But I like brawn in a man. Gives them endurance." Brigit winked slyly.

Some of the others laughed.

"If it's a love charm you want, Brigit," Nila interjected, "find some bog-violet. Bend on your left knee, pluck nine roots, knot them together to make a ring, and place it on your mouth. Then the first man to kiss you will be bound to you."

"There will be no talk of marriage with these men." Mhoire pointed her dagger at Brigit. "They won't be staying, remember?"

"But I don't see why some of them couldn't," Brigit replied. "Even if you chase Drosten off, we could keep a few of the others here. They'd make fine husbands."

"I don't see why you'd want them."

Elanta smiled over at her. "Have you ever been with a man, Mhoire?"

"Of course not."

"Have you never imagined it?"

Mhoire kept her eyes on the ground while she dug into it with her dagger. "I've tried not to imagine it. It's never sounded very pleasant."

"Oh, but it can be. With the right man." Elanta paused. "Kind, handsome ones like that one are the best."

Mhoire looked up and followed the direction of Elanta's gaze. Drosten was approaching the field, dragging a dead deer behind his horse.

She quickly looked down. "That man is one of the most annoying, tyrannical, conceitful men I have ever known." She yanked out a weed and dropped it on the ground.

"And as persistent as a woodpecker," Grainne added. "Unrelenting."

Mhoire nodded vehemently.

"Of course he's persistent," Elanta snorted. "Have you noticed the way he looks at you?"

Mhoire yanked out another weed. "You mean that angry, scornful look?"

"Nay. I mean the one when his eyes go all soft and he looks like he wants to ravish you."

Ravish her? Suddenly, Mhoire was so hot she thought she would faint. She wiped her forehead with the back of her hand. "I don't know what you mean."

"The man's desperate for Dun Darach," Grainne stated flatly. "He'd ravish anything to get it."

Mhoire watched Drosten out of the corner of her eye. Oran had scampered over to him, and he had stopped at her approach and gotten off his horse. Mhoire could hear their voices—the lilt of the child's chattering and the man's patient, deep-toned response.

"You can't deny he's handsome, though," Elanta said.

Indeed, Drosten's form was as straight and solid as a beam of wood. His unkempt locks glinted brightly in the sun, and he gave Oran a wide smile that was utterly guileless and completely charming.

Mhoire looked down at her dagger. "He's fair enough."

"And he's kind to the child."

Mhoire picked up the corner of her apron and wiped a speck of dirt from her blade. "Aye. He's kind to the child."

"They say the Picts are good to their women, too," Elanta went on. "It's the daughter in a royal family that carries the title, you know. Even if a man's in the royal line, like Drosten is, he only gets to be a king if he marries a royal woman. I think that must make them respect women more."

"And so you think Drosten respects women?" Mhoire picked with intense concentration at the bits of dirt that clung to her dagger.

"Well, he does listen to you, Mhoire. He's allowed you to do just about everything you've asked. And he's given you a chance here."

Mhoire's head jerked up. "A chance? You call this a chance?" She gestured to the weedy field that surrounded them. "If Drosten was so respectful of women, he would have been honest with me about Dun Darach. He only gave me this 'chance' because he believed I would fail, that I would have no chance at all. He thinks I'm foolish and incompetent and, no doubt, the most ridiculous woman he's ever encountered." Mhoire's grip tightened on the dagger. Suddenly, she was tired of Elanta's insinuations, tired of all the chatter about men, and tired of being considered an unfeeling idiot. "You think I am out of my wits to reject this man, don't you, Elanta?"

The young woman flushed. "I think you could do worse for a husband."

"I see. Well, let me ask you this. What was your husband like?"

"My husband?"

"Aye. Your husband. Was he a handsome man?"

Elanta looked baffled. "Aye. Why do you ask?"

"Was he a kind man?"

"Aye. Very kind."

"How did you know him?"

"We grew up together. Here, at Dun Darach."

"And you were sweet on him?"

Elanta's blush deepened. "Aye. I was very sweet on him."

"So you wanted to marry him?'

"Aye. I did."

"And if you hadn't, would your father and mother have forced you to?"

Elanta glanced over her shoulder at Nila, who shook her head. She turned back. "Nay. I don't think they would have forced me."

"So you had a choice." Elanta didn't answer. Mhoire pressed. "You had a choice, Elanta, did you not?"

"Aye. I suppose I did."

"And if Brigit married Fergus or if you married Brian, it would be a choice, would it not?" Mhoire waited for Elanta's nod. "That is all I am asking for. A choice. To marry this man or that man or no man at all. But I was given no say in the matter. My father sold me to Drosten for a gold brooch. I know that's the way of it for all the daughters of kings and chieftains. But, tell me this: Would you want that? Would you want to be sold to a man with no thought given to your feelings or desires, just for a piece of gold?"

She stopped speaking and pressed her lips together. But she held Elanta's gaze until the young woman dropped her eyes.

Drosten couldn't help but smile at Oran's lavish praise. She certainly seemed to think he was the greatest hunter of all time, having felled two deer in so many days. She wanted to know all the details: how he had stalked it, where he had shot it, how many other deer he had aimed for and missed before bringing this doe down.

"None."

"None?" Her small mouth fell open.

He grinned. He found himself enjoying her admiration, even though she was just a child. Out of the corner of his eye, though, he was acutely aware of a different female.

As Oran walked around the doe, exclaiming over its

beauty, Drosten positioned himself so he could see Mhoire more directly. He watched her bend to her weeding. She certainly wasn't afraid to get her hands dirty, unlike the other women of standing he had known. If Fionna had seen Mhoire in the fields, she would have called her a peasant. But there wasn't a shred of coarseness about this Irish-woman. The movement of her arms as she handled her dagger was confident but graceful. Her bare calves, which were sticking out from her skirts—unbeknownst to her, Drosten was sure—were firm yet alluringly feminine. In profile, her nose was dainty, the line of her brows fine, and her neck as elegant as that of a swan's. And yet she flung her dagger into the ground with as much precision as a warrior.

Aye, she was a curiosity. Biting but compassionate. Fearful yet willing to take great risks. Combative. Drosten's eyes fell on the quiver of arrows on her back. That was unusual. It would be interesting to see what she could do with those arrows. As long as he wasn't the target.

Drosten shook his head. Damnation, she had a way of slipping into his mind. What poor luck that she didn't have a drop of tender feeling for him.

Drosten's chest heaved. All those women who had cornered him in the banquet halls, who had pursued him shamelessly, who made him feel like a prize stallion instead of an ordinary man, who talked so much and left him so tongue-tied he wanted to bang them over the head—why hadn't he taken a fancy to one of them? Instead of this woman, who no doubt lay abed thinking of ways to get rid of him, if she thought of him at all. But that was part of what he liked about her, he realized. Mhoire never flirted. She spoke to him so straightforwardly it didn't occur to him to feel self-conscious. Aye, she was no seductress. But then, how could it be that she was so enchanting? Drosten raked his hand through his hair. Lord, it hurt his head to think about it.

As he stood there musing, he noticed a change in expression on Mhoire's face. She was upset. He straightened and wondered if he should go over and do something.

He felt Oran tug on his sleeve. "Drosten, how come you're not helping us sow the seed in the fields?"

"Hmm?" He looked down at her absently. She repeated the question.

Drosten hesitated. How much did the child know or understand? "Didn't . . . ah . . . didn't your mother talk to you about this?"

Oran shook her head, sending her hair bouncing.

"Nay? Well . . ." He cleared his throat. "Mhoire and I have this agreement, little one. She and your mother and your grandmother and the others have to try to grow the crops without my help."

"Why?"

Drosten grimaced and then scratched his head. "It's hard to explain, Oran. But Mhoire wants it this way. It's the best thing to do right now."

"Why?"

Drosten closed his eyes briefly, opened them, and blew out a breath. "It's complicated, little one."

"But if we can't do the planting properly, then there won't be enough food."

Drosten's expression softened, and he laid his big hand on the child's small head. "Don't worry, little one. We'll manage."

She looked up at him with round, dark eyes. "You don't want us to have a good harvest, do you?"

Drosten studied her a moment, and then ran his fingers gently over her hair before dropping his hand to his side. "I know it's hard for you to understand this, Oran, but if the crop fails, then Mhoire will have to marry me. And that's what I would like to have happen. But you won't go hungry. I promise you. No one here will go hungry."

"But she won't."

"Won't what?"

"She won't marry you."

Drosten's mouth tightened. "She has to. She gave me her word."

"She'll run away."

Drosten folded his arms across his chest. "She has nowhere to go."

"Then she'll shoot you with her arrows."

He took in a big breath and let it out. "I'll watch my back."

"Then she'll marry Irwin."

"Who?"

"Irwin." Oran raised an arm and pointed. A pale man on a dark horse was trotting across the fields from the north.

Drosten stiffened, as alert as a hawk. "Who is he?"

"He's our neighbor. I don't like him."

Drosten's eyes followed Irwin's passage. "I don't like him either."

"Maybe Mhoire will." Oran tugged on his sleeve again. "You'd better kiss her."

"What?" Drosten turned and gaped down at Oran.

"Kiss her." She nodded emphatically. "People always get married after they kiss each other."

Drosten looked over at Mhoire. She had gotten to her feet and was eyeing Irwin's approach. "It's not that simple, little one."

As they watched, Brigit leaned toward Mhoire and said something. Mhoire laid her knife on the ground and smoothed down her gown. Then she patted her hair.

Oran tugged on his sleeve. "You'd better kiss her *now*."

"Well, she's not going to kiss that fool." Then he charged across the field, leaving Oran and his horse behind.

Chapter Nine

Irwin of Kingarth was an average-sized man with bony shoulders that drooped toward his chest and wispy hair the color of old carrots. A large nose splayed above thin, pale lips.

He stopped his horse a few feet from where Mhoire was standing. "You are Mhoire ni Colman?"

She cast an admiring eye over his dark red tunic, embroidered with yellow thread. "I am."

"Irwin of Kingarth. My holding is the next one to the north." His glance darted over her, pausing an extra moment on the bow that she held in her hand. "You have taken up residence at Dun Darach?"

"Aye. My mother was born here."

Drosten strode up and planted himself next to her.

"And you are, sir?"

"Drosten mac Gormach."

"From Pictland?"

"Aye."

"I heard this Irishwoman was betrothed to a Pict."

"Not yet betrothed," Mhoire announced.

"Not yet?"

"But we will be soon," Drosten growled.

"Not necessarily," Mhoire noted.

Drosten lowered his head like a bull. A small bead of sweat broke out on Mhoire's upper lip.

"Do you have your crops in the ground, Irwin?" Brigit called out.

"Aye," Irwin responded. "All the crops are in."

"What did you plant?" Elanta inquired.

"Ten fields of oats, ten fields of barley, ten fields of rye. Five fields of turnips, five of carrots, five of leeks, three of parsnips. And a mixed field of garlic and onions and some other things."

Mhoire blinked. The man must own a huge amount of land. "You have good soil then?" she asked.

Elanta answered. "Irwin has excellent land. Very productive." She smiled at Irwin, and his thin lips turned up.

Mhoire studied him. He wasn't bad looking. True, he didn't appear very strong, but his face had no blemishes. "Your clan has lived here long?" she asked.

"We've been in Dal Riata for two hundred years. And in all that time," he said awkwardly, "I doubt we have ever had a more beautiful neighbor."

Mhoire blushed. No one had ever paid her such a direct and public compliment. She smiled and glanced around at the others. Grainne was frowning heavily. Brigit and Elanta were both looking as satisfied as a cat that had just planted a mouse at its owner's feet. Nila was watching Drosten, who, Mhoire realized with horror as she followed Nila's gaze, appeared ready to haul Irwin off his horse and bash his head in. Just as she sprang forward to intercede, a high scream pierced the air.

Drosten leapt toward the sound and pulled out his dagger.

Little one!

Oran screamed again, from across the field, a high-pitched wail of terror. A boar charged toward her on short powerful legs. Drosten's horse whinnied loudly and reared. But Oran was frozen to the spot, stiff as a cadaver, her eyes huge with fright. Drosten cursed himself for leaving her alone and for forgetting his spear, which was holstered to his horse. All he had on him was the dagger. If he couldn't stop the boar with that, he would have to wrestle it to the ground.

If only the horse would stay put, he prayed. If only he could get to Oran and throw her on its saddle. But despite pouring every bit of speed he possessed into his legs, he knew the animal would reach the child before he did. He had to throw the dagger. Now. Dropping to one knee, Drosten pulled back on his arm and took aim at the boar's fleshy neck.

He sensed something whiz past his ear just before he flung his knife. An arrow pierced the boar's hide, and the animal stopped in its tracks. Up and running again, Drosten saw a second arrow puncture the animal's eye. The boar fell to the ground at Oran's feet just as Drosten reached her and scooped her up in his arms.

She was out of her mind with fear, howling like a wild thing, her eyes round and flooded with tears. She didn't recognize him. Screaming, she pulled away from his hold with all her small might. But he dared not let her go for fear that she would run off into the woods and hurt herself. Gasping for breath, Drosten gripped the child to his chest. She pummeled his head with her fists and kicked at his stomach.

"Oran!"

He turned at Elanta's cry and saw her and the others running toward him.

Tears streamed down Elanta's face as he lowered the wailing Oran into her arms. *How could I have been so stupid?* Drosten asked himself. *How could I have left the child alone? Of all the senseless, irresponsible things to do! What an idiot I am.*

Drosten felt a touch on his arm and looked down into Mhoire's concerned face. "Are you hurt?" she asked. He didn't understand her question. She smiled slightly. "You took quite a banging."

He shook his head numbly.

Irwin's reedy voice broke out. "Do you do this often,

lady, or was this a lucky shot?" He stood next to the boar's carcass, his eyes on the arrows buried in its flesh.

Drosten noted Irwin's arsenal of weapons and wondered why a man on a horse hadn't gotten to Oran sooner than a man running. Fury burned in his gut.

"Someone has taught you to use a bow," Irwin continued. "How peculiar."

Mhoire's chin went up. "I know how to defend myself and others. Is that so very odd?"

"Usually a woman relies on a man to defend her."

"A man is not always available."

"A smart man would always be available to a woman like you. And fighting is a man's task, is it not?"

Drosten flinched. He glanced at Mhoire, saw her cheeks turn scarlet, and knew that Irwin's words had stung. He flexed his fists. Drained or not, he was going to have to hit the man.

Mhoire reached Irwin before he did. She pulled an arrow from her quiver and held the point level with Irwin's nose. "I have saved this child's life with these arrows and killed our supper. I consider that a worthwhile activity." She lowered her arm. "Ordinarily, I would offer you the hospitality of my hearth, but I can see you would be most unhappy breaking bread with a woman as wild and uncouth as I am. So good day to you, sir."

Irwin blinked rapidly. "I did not mean to offend, lady."

A sad expression flitted across Mhoire's face. Then it hardened into an angry stare that proved as lethal as her bow. Silently, Irwin climbed onto his horse and trotted off.

Chapter Ten

Early the next morning, Mhoire slung her quiver onto her back and set off to explore the woodlands that draped the slopes east of Dun Darach. She suspected they were full of squirrels, rabbits, fox, and other small animals, and she was eager to bring some of the game back to the fort for supper.

She was also determined not to let Irwin's words distress her. It was an unusually fair day, full of sweet air and fleecy clouds. *We must have more days like this one,* Mhoire thought to herself. *Good growing days.* It was late in the season to be planting—past Easter—and they would need plenty of fair weather to bring the crops to harvest.

The blue skies coaxed out the forest creatures, and by midmorning, Mhoire had felled ten plump rabbits, which she strung together on a sinew cord and carried across her shoulders.

Striding across an open meadow, she tugged at the collar of her gown, opening the laces from her throat to her waist and exposing her thin linen undershirt. Her hair was bothering her, too. It needed to either be bound tighter so it wouldn't wobble as she walked, or not bound at all. She slipped out her hair pin, and let the dark waves fall about her shoulders.

She thought of the old blind harper who used to come to her father's hall. When he lifted his voice and poured out a melody, his dull eyes turned radiant, as if the act of singing unfettered his sight and made him a different man. That's how Mhoire felt now, walking among the hills, alone but for the birds and the buttercups. All the defenses she had constructed, the protective walls of silence and conformity, disappeared. The sun warmed her shoulders like a mantle, and the pure, greening freshness made her blood sing.

At the edge of the meadow was a small bower of sycamore trees, and she made her way toward the dappled shade. She laid her string of rabbits on the ground near the largest tree, still vital despite a trunk that was completely split, and wiped her forehead with her sleeve. Then she leaned against the tree's rough side and lifted her face to the gentle breeze that sifted through its branches. Archery cleansed her like a tonic. When she took aim at a target, her worries and doubts fell away like sediment drifting to the bottom of a pond.

A movement on the ground caught her eye, and a large rabbit hopped into the circle of trees. Mhoire slipped an arrow from her quiver and raised her bow. She held her breath and then released the bowstring. *Got it!*

"I see the rabbit population isn't safe in this holding."

Mhoire spun around. Drosten was leaning against a tree trunk, smiling, with a club in his hand and a bow slung over his shoulder.

Her heart jumped and then lodged itself high in her throat. "I . . . had intended to take some squirrels. But the rabbits have more meat on their bones."

His smile widened into a grin. "And it looks like I will be spending the evening making supper out of them. If I remember our agreement correctly." He held up his own string. Hanging from it were just two rabbits.

"Are you a good cook?" she asked impishly.

"I suspect I'll become one."

She laughed at that, a merry sound like the tinkling of bells.

Suddenly, just beyond Drosten, another rabbit leapt out from a small bush. Mhoire seized an arrow from her quiver and with one swift movement, notched it to her bow and fired. It caught the animal in the neck.

She wrinkled her brow and stared at the creature—shocked, not by her aim but by the fact that she had acted so impulsively. *He will think I am boastful.* Self-consciously, she walked over to the rabbit to retrieve her arrow.

She glanced at Drosten as she passed him. He was watching her closely, a half-smile on his face. When she passed him a second time to collect the arrow from the other rabbit she had killed, he was wearing the same expression.

"You're making my nerves jump," she grumbled.

"If that's how you shoot when your nerves jump, I'd like to see what happens when they're calm."

Mhoire's frown deepened, and her face burned. It was shameful to be caught hunting like this, with her hair down and her gown half-open. And now he was mocking her. But she was not going to defend herself to him as she had to Irwin. *If he thinks I'm a crazy woman, so be it.*

She pulled a strip of cloth from under her belt and concentrated on cleaning the blood from her arrows. Drosten ambled up to her, slipped his own bow off his shoulder, and dropped it on the ground, along with his club. Then he nodded at the weapon that was hanging from her shoulder. "May I look at that?"

She slipped the bow off her arm and handed it to him, carefully avoiding his eyes.

He ran his large hand over the wood. Then he fingered the string. He shifted the bow to one hand and assessed its weight. Finally, he pulled back on the string and lifted the weapon as if to shoot, taking imaginary aim at one of the gnarled old sycamores. Then he lowered the bow and ran his fingers over its curves once more.

"It's very light."

Mhoire peeped at him from under her lashes. He didn't seem to be taunting her after all. In fact, he appeared curious. "I . . . couldn't hold steady the bows made of yew. They were too heavy. So I made this one out of rowan."

"You made this?"

"Aye."

He made a little grunting noise and stroked the weapon from one smooth end to the other. "Good work."

She leaned toward him a little. "See the strings?" He glanced at her and then studied the bow again. "They're made from gut rather than tree bast. Gut is much more consistent."

He raised the bow again for another imaginary shot. "It is certainly effective." He looked squarely at her and grinned. "But I'd say it's the aim of the archer that makes this weapon work so well."

She reddened once more.

Drosten leaned the bow against the trunk of the nearest tree and then relaxed against it himself, folding his arms. Mhoire slipped the two clean arrows into her quiver.

"Tell me," he said, studying her, "did you shoot that boar standing or on one knee?"

She tucked the bloody rag back under her belt and faced him. He looked like a prince from an ancient legend, with his sunlit hair and his yellow tunic and his silver-clasped belt.

"I took the first shot standing. But for the second one, I knelt. I wanted to be sure I hit the target."

A dark cloud seemed to drift across his face. "I should never have left the child alone."

"What happened with Oran wasn't your fault, Drosten."

He tightened his arms against his chest. "The boar smelled the blood from the deer I killed. I should have realized the danger in the situation."

"Don't blame yourself."

A muscle in his face tensed.

Mhoire hesitated, wanting to convince him of his innocence but not knowing how. Biting her lip, she turned and walked back to where one of the dead rabbits was lying on the ground. "You know," she said in a lighter tone, "it was probably your dagger that killed the beast, not my arrow."

"Ah. Not only are you an excellent archer, but you are humble, too."

She looked over her shoulder and saw that he was smiling again.

She busied herself attaching the rabbit to her string. She felt awkward, alone with Drosten like this, discussing an ability that everyone else thought was horrifying. But his presence was surprisingly agreeable today, and she found she did not want to break away from it. His frowns had disappeared, and his demeanor was courteous. More than courteous. Or maybe the sunshine had mellowed her. Whatever the cause, talking with him now was like having one more beaker of mead when you were already besotted. Pleasant. So pleasant that one was inclined not to give thought to the consequences.

"Tell me about Scathach."

"What?"

"Scathach. The warrior woman. Tell me about her."

"Are you mocking me?"

Drosten grinned. "Not with that bow nearby."

She blushed again and cursed herself for it. She feared that by the time this encounter was over, her face would be permanently red.

"Tell me," he prompted again.

"Well—" Mhoire walked toward the other rabbit. "Scathach was a great teacher. She knew all the magical arts of war." She picked up the animal and began to thread the string through the skin just under the shoulder joint. "Scathach could jump on top of a lance and ride it without falling off. She could make this terrible scream that paralyzed whoever heard it. And, of course, she knew all the arts of swordplay and archery and hurling. All the best warriors asked to train with her. Like Cuchulain. He was Ireland's greatest hero. When most people hear the bard's tales, they remember Cuchulain and his deeds. But Scathach—she taught Cuchulain, and she was a seer, as well."

"Ah. To be able to defend yourself against all enemies and to know the future, too—that would make a person quite formidable." He paused. "Is that how you would like to be?"

Mhoire pulled the rabbit tight against the others and looked up. He was still eyeing her keenly but without mockery. "I have no desire to be fearsome. But I would like to be able to defend myself."

"You can defend yourself. I have no doubt that you could shoot a man as easily as you shoot a rabbit. Men are much bigger targets and they don't move nearly as fast. Haven't you ever done it?"

"Shot a man? Nay!"

"Hmm. Just targets and game?"

"Aye. And rarely game at that. There was never much need at home, and I . . . I couldn't let others know that I was doing this."

"Your father and mother didn't approve. Is that what you mean?"

Mhoire looked down at the rabbits and stroked their fur to cover up her embarrassment. "They forbade it. My father saw me practicing once and he said I must never touch a weapon again. He said weapons were for men. Clearly, he had forgotten all the ancient legends. And history. It has only been a hundred years since King Brude declared that women did not have to fight beside men in battle."

"You disobeyed your father then."

"Aye."

"Who taught you?"

"No one. I couldn't ask any of my father's men for instruction because he would have punished them. I just watched the warriors in the courtyard and then I went off and tried to hit things in the woods."

"Show me what you know."

"What?" Her head bobbed up.

Drosten picked up her bow and held it out. "Tell me a few of your secrets, Scathach."

She could scarce believe what he was asking. "But you are already a very good warrior."

He pushed himself away from the sycamore trunk and

with two strides was standing before her. His eyes danced. "Come. Show me how you do it. My rabbit-hunting skills need improvement."

She hesitated, all confusion. To have her interest in archery discovered was one thing, but to demonstrate . . . She bit her lip and reached for the weapon.

At first haltingly and then with more and more enthusiasm, she showed Drosten how she grasped the bow, how she took her aim, and how she released the bowstring.

"Can you see that?" She turned to him. But he was looking at her face, not her fingers.

"I see that," he murmured.

The warmth in his eyes unsettled her. "You . . . you should try it yourself. Before you forget."

"Aye, I should."

He reached out. Still under the spell of his gaze, she started to hand her weapon to him. Then her wits returned. "Nay," she said abruptly, drawing the bow back. "You must use your own bow. That would be better."

He nodded and picked up his weapon. Then he notched an arrow on the string and looked at her. "Target?"

She scanned the countryside beyond him. "That tree there."

He followed her gaze and squinted. The tree was at least fifty yards away. "Hmm."

He raised the weapon, released the string, and missed.

He grimaced fiercely. "That was very good," Mhoire pronounced. "You almost hit the target." He peered down at her out of the corner of his eye.

She ignored the skepticism she saw there. "Take another arrow, and let me watch more closely."

He did as she told him.

She peered at his hands and then moved behind him. Standing on her toes, she tried to observe his sight line. But he was so much taller than she was that she couldn't see the relationship between his eyes and his hands.

"Perhaps you should kneel. I can't get a proper look at what you're doing."

He got down on one knee and took aim again.

Still behind him, she straddled his leg and bent one knee herself until her head was at the same level as his. She had to reach out as far as she could to get around his broad shoulder with her left hand. The length of her arm lay against his, and she could feel the bulge of his muscle under the cloth of his tunic. Her heart began to beat as swiftly as a rabbit's. *Ease yourself,* she ordered. *You're just showing him how to hold the bow.* But she had never been this close to a man before, and her body vibrated with awareness.

Tentatively, she pried his fingers open. "Move your fingers a little farther apart. Like this."

His fingers were warm and rough under hers. All of him was warm and rough. Except for his hair, which she inadvertently brushed with her nose and which was as smooth as the silk of a milkweed pod.

She glanced at his face, an inch from her own. He looked slightly pained, and his eyes were shut. Alarm rushed through her. "Are you all right?"

"Fine."

"You must keep your eyes open, Drosten."

"I know that." He gritted his teeth and opened his eyes.

The top of his tunic was untied, and a delicious heat emanated from underneath it. His neck smelled of sweat and the sun.

She reached around his right side and, with her right hand, lightly touched his where it held the bowstring. Her breasts, barely covered by her undershirt, pressed into his back.

"Mhoire," he croaked.

"What is it?" She leaned even closer so she could look around his shoulder and see his face.

His eyes were shut again. "We'd better get on with this lesson."

"Are you certain you are not ill? You look most strange."

"I'm not ill."

"But you must keep your eyes open, Drosten." He opened his eyes. "Remember," she spoke softly into his ear, "relax your back as you aim." She laid her right hand against the small of his back and spread her fingers. "Just before you release the bowstring, loosen your back." She dug her fingertips into the muscle around his spine and kneaded. His bones were as true as a ship's mast and the muscles hard as iron. "Then—" She lifted her hand and ran it lightly along the length of his right arm till she felt the warm, bare skin of his taut wrist. "—keep this arm straight after the release so the arrow doesn't veer. That's the most important part." She leaned back on her heels. "Now shoot."

His arrow hit the tree.

"Very good!"

He shook his head. "That was a miracle."

"But you have much talent, Drosten."

He ran his free hand through his hair and half-turned to look at her. Amusement shone in his eyes. "Not under these conditions."

Her brow wrinkled. "What conditions?"

He laughed. Then he bounded to his feet and held out a hand, leaving his bow on the ground. "Come. I owe you something for your instruction."

She grasped his outstretched hand and let him pull her to her feet. Suddenly, she was close to him again, the length and breadth of his body filling the sun-splattered space before her. She stared up at him, and longing rose in her, as full and deep as the tide.

She arched toward him. It took all of her will not to reach up and sink her hands into the hair that curled at the nape of his neck, to bring her mouth to his.

"What do you wish to learn?" he murmured. His pupils glowed with intensity.

She remained mute.

"I'd show you how to kill a man, but I think one look from your eyes would do that."

With a sharp intake of breath, she stepped back, confounded and hurt. "What do you mean?"

He simply shook his head.

She folded her arms tightly across her chest and looked away.

He muttered something.

"What did you say?" she asked sharply.

He shook his head again. "It doesn't matter."

Neither of them looked at the other.

"Elanta says it's the old language you speak." She cast about for words, anything to cover up the discomfort she was feeling.

"Aye, sometimes. But I'm not always aware of it."

"All . . . all your men speak it, do they?"

"It's the language we learned as children."

"But you know Gaelic."

"The monks taught us Gaelic. Everyone in Pictland speaks Gaelic now." He glanced at her. "Does it bother you? The old language?"

"Nay." She caught his eye briefly, and looked away. "I . . . I just didn't know about it. I've led a sheltered life, you see." She looked down at the ground. "There is much I don't know."

He was quiet for a moment. A breeze drifted through the bower of trees, and the branches of the sycamores squeaked.

"Well, I'd best show you a few things then, *mo milidh.*"

My warrior. The words would have been mocking, had the tone not been so gentle.

He walked over to where his weapons were lying on the ground and picked up his club. "Let's pretend this is a sword." He held the club out to her hilt-first.

She grasped it in her right hand. "What are we doing?"

"I'm telling you my battle secrets. Now come at me with the weapon. As if it were a sword."

She blinked a few times. She didn't understand why he was doing this, but at least his eyes no longer held that smoldering look that wrenched feelings from her she didn't even know she had.

She gripped the club firmly and made a thrust to his stomach.

He grabbed the shaft. "Just what I thought." He released the weapon. "Hold it in both hands."

Mhoire did as he instructed. "Like this?"

"Aye. Now come at me again, but here." With the edge of his hand, he made a slicing motion against the left side of his neck where it joined his shoulder. "It's an easy spot to hit, and most of the time it's a fatal blow. Bring your sword up with both hands and then down, and the weight of the weapon will give you extra force."

She stared at his neck and grimaced. She wasn't accustomed to hitting people.

"Come," he commanded.

She raised the club and swung it. Once again, he caught the weapon before it hit him.

He frowned. "That's difficult for you, isn't it?"

"Aye. I'm not very strong."

"You're very strong for a woman. But these weapons are heavy and I'm a big man." He scrutinized her. "Let's try your dagger."

She started to slip her small eating dagger from the sheath at her waist. "Not that one," he said. "The other one."

She stilled. "What other one?"

A half-smile touched his lips. "I don't know where it is, but I know you have another dagger on you somewhere. I saw you hack your way through a roof with it. Remember?"

Flushing, she turned to one side, lifted her skirt, and drew the dagger out of the sheath that was strapped to her leg. It was considerably larger than the one at her waist.

"Good. Now show me how you hold it."

She clutched the dagger tightly in her fist. He reached out as if to touch her hand, but stopped himself. Instead, he made a circular gesture. "Reverse your hold. Lay the hilt in the palm of your hand."

She looked up at him in surprise. "That doesn't seem right."

"It is right. I'll show you why. Lay the hilt in the palm of your hand and then wrap your fingers around it."

She did so. It felt peculiar. She raised her elbow and tried to plunge the dagger downward, but the movement was ungainly. "I can't swing it this way."

"You can if you come from below, not from above like that. Keep your elbow close to your body and your arm low. Then go for my gut. In and up. One smooth movement. Your small size will help you. Just move right into me." He took two steps backward. "Now."

"I'm not going to stab you."

"Nay, you're not. But you're going to try."

"I am not."

"Aye, you are. You need to know this, Mhoire. If you want to be a warrior, then behave like one."

She lunged at him.

Just before the knife hit his flesh, he gripped her wrist. And then his other arm snapped around her waist, pressing her body against his. Startled by the strength and quickness of his movement, she gaped wide-eyed into his face.

She pushed back against his arm with all her might but it was as unyielding as an iron bar. Panic rose in her throat like vomit, and she screamed.

Drosten dropped his hold instantly, and she stumbled backward, letting the dagger fall.

"I'm sorry, Mhoire. I didn't mean to frighten you. I'm sorry."

She covered her face with her hands. Her fear was a caged animal, and in one leap it had escaped and shamed her.

He took an awkward step toward her. "Forgive me. I shouldn't have touched you."

She moved her trembling fingers from her face to her hair and smoothed it back from her brow. "I must go. I'm not hurt. But I must go."

Drosten watched her agitated movements as she walked over to where her things were lying on the ground. Clumsily, she concealed her dagger under her skirt. She slid the bow over her shoulder, picked up the heavy string of game, dropped it, and picked it up again. Drosten turned to the sycamore tree, lay a bent arm against its trunk, and buried his face in his sleeve.

That was how Grainne found them.

Her long face screwed up in consternation when she halted at the edge of the grove. "What has happened?"

Mhoire came toward her with a closed expression. "Nothing."

Drosten raised his head and pulled away from the tree.

Grainne scrutinized one and then the other. But she kept her thoughts to herself.

"I came looking for you, Mhoire, to tell you that the cow is here."

Mhoire nodded.

"What cow?" Drosten asked.

"I bought a cow from Irwin," Mhoire replied. "We need milk for the child, and butter and cheese."

"You bought a cow from Irwin?"

"Aye. He has plenty of cows. And he is willing to help us. He is one of our people."

"Not a Pict, you mean."

Mhoire didn't respond.

"And what did you pay for this cow?"

"I traded him a silver hair pin for it."

"I see." Drosten picked up his bow with one hand and his club with the other. "Irwin has a use for hairpins, does he?" Without looking at her, he strode away.

Mhoire watched his back as he receded over the side of the hill, her insides tight and aching.

"There's something else," Grainne said, placing a bony hand on her arm. Mhoire heard the rasp of fear in her voice. "Your father is at the fort."

Chapter Eleven

Grainne's words squeezed Mhoire's heart like a fist.

"Is my father angry?"

One look at her friend's face told her the answer.

Of course Colman was furious. By refusing to marry Drosten, Mhoire had denied his wishes in the boldest way possible. She had prayed—beyond all reason—that he would not confront her in person. But here he was.

"I must go and greet him."

Grainne's hand tightened on her arm. "You could hide in the cave. I could tell him that I couldn't find you. He will think you have gotten lost. Or maybe that you have been kidnapped . . ."

"He would find me somehow."

Grainne dropped her hand.

They made their way down the hill and waded through the high grasses toward the fort. Mhoire struggled to order her thoughts, but they were as slippery as eels and just as formless. There was no argument that could justify a daughter ignoring her father's commands in order to live on her own in another country.

They ascended the bank that led to the break in the wall where the gate had once been. Mhoire glanced at Grainne, who was trudging beside her, head down, in her awkward, stumbling gait. "You'll stay with me?"

Grainne looked at her, her eyes dark and agonized. "Of course I will. I'll stay right by you."

Mhoire ran her perspiring hands over her skirt and stepped through the gaping hole in the wall. Her father faced her across the courtyard.

"You look like a whore," he said.

In three steps he was before her, and she stared into his pale, hazel eyes. She hated his eyes. They were always changing color. Today they were a watery green, the hue of a wrathful sea.

She clutched at the open neck of her gown and pulled the cloth together. "God be with you, Father."

He struck her hand, batting it from her chest. "You have no shame," he hissed. "Do not pretend you do."

She began to tremble. Colman was full of drink and coiled taut like a serpent. This was the worst he could be. The very worst.

His eyes raked her from head to toe. Sweat pooled in her armpits and trickled down her sides. *Why hadn't she put her hair back up? Why hadn't she fixed her gown?*

"You are too much like your mother."

His gaze shifted to the string of game that she held in her hand and the bow that was slung over her shoulder. "Drop those things."

She let the string of rabbits fall to the ground. It took all her will to uncurl her fingers from her bow and place it beside them.

"Why are you not married?"

"I have made an agreement with the Picts. . . "

"*You* made an agreement with the Picts? *I* made an agreement! You have no authority to deal with them!"

Mhoire wiped her wet hands on her gown. "The Picts have agreed to let me try to make my way alone here, and if I succeed, they will release me from the marriage contract."

"Release you? Never! You disobedient, willful child! I make the contracts! I decide *whom* you will marry and *when* you will marry! You will marry one of these Pictish heathens and that is that!"

He took a step closer to her. She stepped backward.

"I could not believe it when I got the message from Gormach mac Nechtan! The marriage was delayed, he said. You had returned the brooch, he said. You thieving child! Look at me!"

Slowly, she raised her eyes. Colman's face had gone white as a demon's. He was out of his mind with fury now. Out of the corner of her eye, she noticed that some of Drosten's men were clustered near the gathering hall. A few of the women had crept into the courtyard as well. Mhoire knew none of them would intervene. It was a father's right to do as he pleased with his children.

"How did you get the brooch?"

"You . . . I . . . It was in your room. You were drunk."

"I'm never drunk!" Wildness glazed his eyes.

She loathed him. His weak spirit. His cruel impulses. His hollow soul. "You were drunk, as you are drunk every night."

There. She had said it.

Colman's eyes bulged. "I have plans here! You will not alter them! Do you hear me? It is your duty to do as I wish! It is your duty to obey me!"

"And what about your duty, Father? Did you do your duty to these suffering, starving women?"

His arm whipped up, and he struck her hard across the cheek.

She staggered and tasted the metallic flavor of blood on her lips. Grainne hurled herself at Colman and grabbed his arm. With one furious movement, he flung her off and she crashed onto the ground.

Mhoire fell to her knees beside her friend. Everything before her faded, as if snow were falling, and a roaring sound filled her ears.

Then she heard a yell. She looked up and saw Drosten grab Colman by the shoulders and pin him against the rubble wall.

"Stop! Please, stop!" Mhoire's words came out in a sob. Drosten turned. She sent a silent plea with her pain-filled eyes.

"Hold onto him," Drosten grumbled to Alfred. Then he strode over to Mhoire and dropped to his knees before her.

She was shaking from head to foot, like a leaf in the wind.

"Please . . . don't fight. I can't . . . bear it." Colman frightened her to the bone. But to subdue him with violence would terrify her even more.

"Can you make him go away?" she said.

Drosten was silent.

Mhoire knew he was struggling. His sense of justice had been honed on countless battlefields and was far simpler than hers.

She squeezed her eyes shut, willing him to do as she asked.

Finally, he let out a low, deep groan. "Aye. I can make him go away. Far away."

Mhoire slumped in relief, and Grainne's strong arm fell across her shoulders.

The sun was sinking heavily, like a dull blade into a carcass, when Drosten laid his forearms atop the sagging courtyard wall and leaned into the cold stone. A sickly orange glow lit the rim of the western sky. The sea—a muddy gray—heaved and fell, heaved and fell.

He had sent four men with Colman to see that he got back in his boat and returned to Ireland. It had taken every shred of Drosten's self-control not to throw the man into the sea. But he had made a promise to Mhoire, and he would keep it, at least for now. He had made sure, though, that Colman would not forget the feel of his fist. And he assured him that if he ever raised a hand against Mhoire again, retaliation would be swift and fatal, no matter how hard his daughter begged for his worthless life.

Then he had assembled the rest of his men and gave them their orders. Never was Mhoire to be alone. It would be the job of two men, each day, to keep her in sight. Their job was to protect her, and if any of them failed in that task, Drosten himself would dole out the consequences.

So this was why she wanted Dun Darach. This was why she resisted marriage. Why she had dared confront his father. Why she had clutched at his offer to let her try a life on her own. Why she was so damned desperate. Her ambitions had seemed foolish to him. And now—now they were undeniable. A man like Colman could turn his rage on her at any time, with tragic consequences.

No wonder she had recoiled at his touch that morning. If this was her experience of men, how could she not be terrified?

Drosten scanned the horizon, which was fast disappearing under the blanket of night. What in God's own world was he going to do? She wanted Dun Darach for herself, but he could not give it up. This was his people's last hope—a fortress on the coast, an alliance with the Scots, a united force against the Danes. The Danes were gutting his country the way a hunter eviscerates a deer. They had to be stopped. And the Britons as well. Drosten knew, as surely as he knew his own name, that between the merciless onslaught of the Danes and the relentless, sneaking attacks of the Britons, the entire Pictish society could be wiped out.

Nay, he must have Dun Darach. He must marry Mhoire. They must continue on the course they had set themselves upon. He would let her keep trying in this pitiful way to coax a crop out of Dun Darach's hard land. And when she failed, they would marry. She would be desolate but resigned. He would be victorious and miserable. How could he not be, living side by side with a woman who undoubtedly believed all men were villains?

Drosten covered his face with his hands, and in his mind's eye he saw Mhoire as she had been that morning. Laughing. Smiling. And she was so good with that bow. So true. It was astonishing, what she had taught herself. What she had held onto, in secret. And the way she had touched him. So hesitant, so innocent, so gentle. It had been such sweet torture to have her fingers push against his, to feel the tickle of her breath against his neck, to know that with a turn of his head he could reach her soft mouth.

And then he had ruined it, with his flip comment and his impetuous clench that had frightened her out of her wits. Drosten raked his hand through his hair. *Nay, it was not him.* It was that damned father of hers! Colman had ruined Mhoire the way the Danes had ruined Dun Darach. The pity was, he knew how to rebuild a fort. He had no idea how to heal a woman's soul.

His stomach rumbled, reminding him that he had not eaten since he had broken fast that morning. He wasn't hungry. Far from it. But he pushed himself away from the wall. His years as a wandering warrior had taught him to eat whether he wanted to or not.

Piles of wreckage loomed gray and spectral as he made his way across the courtyard to the gathering hall. Wearily, he stepped across the threshold. The hall was quiet and dim, except for a pool of light cast by a low fire in the center of the room.

He had thought the day could not batter him with any more emotion, but then he saw Mhoire, huddled on a log before the fire, her head hanging low and her hair falling across her face in long, chaotic tendrils.

She looked like a rag doll: forlorn, broken, and abandoned. But it was the way she clutched her bow that shattered him.

She raised her head, and her hands tensed on the weapon. Then she recognized him and lowered her eyes to the hearth.

He approached her silently. Outside the perimeter of light, he could see that a number of his men—most likely those who would be standing watch later that night—were stretched out on their blankets. On the other side of the hall, some of the women were asleep as well. A few sat with their backs against the wall, but none were talking now.

He squatted beside Mhoire and looked up into her face. A purple bruise stained her left cheek. She held herself rigidly, a sign, Drosten knew, of pain. And she was trembling ever so slightly. He recognized that sign as well, for he had seen it often in his younger soldiers. Battle shock.

"You should get some sleep, Mhoire."

Her eyes glistened in the firelight.

"He won't be back, I promise you."

"How do you know?" Her voice was barely audible.

He wished he could tell her the truth—that he had thrashed the man to unconsciousness before throwing him over a horse. But he didn't want to speak to her of violence. Not tonight. "I sent him off with four of my best men. And I have sentries posted all around the fort."

She swallowed hard. The golden light of the fire flared on her delicate throat. "He's ruthless."

"So am I." He leaned toward her, longing to pull her into his arms and gather her safe against him. But he could only console her with his words. "I won't let him hurt you."

"I was wrong to defy him."

Drosten's jaw clenched. "Mayhap. But he was wrong to hit you."

"Was he?"

"Hitting a woman is the act of a coward."

Her lips turned up in a mockery of a smile. "He is the king of cowards then."

Drosten scanned her strained face. "Your mother?"

"I believe so," she whispered.

The fire snapped and spit. A burning log split in two with a whispered thud, and a small burst of sparks floated upwards.

"Sometimes he would go . . . wild. After my mother died, I knew it could just be a matter of time before he raised his hand to me. Some imagined slight—a dish not cooked to his liking, or the fire not high enough. And then one evening he told me that he was going to send me here. To Dun Darach." She turned and looked at Drosten, wonderment in her voice. "I thought to myself, this is a gift from God."

Her words ended on a quaver, like a sparrow's lament.

Drosten hung his head. *Dun Darach was her gift from God. And he must snatch it away.* He listened to the fire for a moment, and the sound of Mhoire's careful, trembling breaths.

"You can protect yourself from him now, Mhoire. If you try."

She looked at her bow and flexed her fingers against its smooth curves. "Aye. I think I could now. If I prepare for it. Now that I know what he might do."

"You've no need to worry tonight. Lay down here by the fire. I'll stay awake."

"I'm not tired."

He knew that was a lie. But he didn't argue.

Drosten stood, walked over to where his pack was tucked against the wall, and pulled out his blanket, a length of plain brown wool. He walked back to Mhoire and held it out to her. "Take this. In case you get cold."

She looked at it, and then glanced at the ground beside her. "I have my own," she said. He saw it then, a green cloth folded into a neat square.

He left her gazing vacantly into the embers, and instead of taking his usual solitary place outside, he sank against the stone wall near his men. Upright all night, he dozed and he woke, and he dozed and he woke. At some point, in the deepest part of the night, he saw that she had laid down on her side and fallen asleep, her bow still clutched in her hands. And he realized that the ache in his belly was too profound to be caused by lack of food.

Chapter Twelve

"So you're telling me that there's a woman in charge?"

"Not exactly in charge, Your Highness."

"Exactly what, then?"

A trickle of sweat slid from the man's brow. "She just thinks she's in charge, my liege."

A heavy eyebrow lifted the golden crown a fraction of an inch. "My friend, don't you know you should never let a woman think she's in charge? She'll create more havoc than a ferret trapped in your breeches."

Snickers bounced off the embroidered wall hangings. The raftered hall, the centerpiece of the royal fort of Dun Add, was filled with the men of the king's court, dressed in silken tunics and shaggy fleece cloaks.

"Things aren't going the way I planned, my liege."

"Apparently not." The king of Dal Riata picked an oyster from a silver platter that a page held before him.

"The woman is wayward, my liege."

"Wayward women do not interest me." The king drank a large mouthful of wine, and wiped his chin with his sleeve. Then he leveled his gaze at the man before him. "I do, on the other hand, care about the Pictish prince. He is dangerous. And there is only one way to stop him."

"I need time, Your Highness."

"I've given you time. I've stayed away from Dun Darach while you made your plans. Now time is running out."

"Then give me an army."

"An army? You can't take care of two score men and a handful of scrawny women without an army?"

The hall tittered.

"I can. But if you want speed—"

"I want results. You have Drosten mac Gormach in your lap. Deal with him."

The page slipped to the king's other side and presented him with a tray of spice cakes. The king selected one and pushed it into his mouth. "As for the woman, she's not a blood relation. Kill her or take her for yourself. But whatever you do, for Mary's sake, be subtle. I don't want to start a war with the Picts."

The king leaned back and closed his eyes. The man opened his mouth as if to speak, thought better of it, and backed into the shadows.

It was just before dawn when Mhoire awakened. She had dreamt all night. But not of the man who slapped and humiliated her. She dreamt of the other one. Whose warmth threatened to melt the walls she had so carefully erected inside herself. Walls she must keep up.

She pushed herself to her knees, reached for the leather bundle that held her personal things, and drew out a small object. Cradling it in her palm, she tiptoed past the sleeping bodies scattered around the hall, pulled open the heavy oak door, and stepped into the courtyard.

The air was thick and the sky lowered, smothering the light like a lid on a box.

Shadows separated from the gloom. She tensed but quickly recognized the shapes as two of Drosten's warriors. Then she sensed movement behind her.

"Mhoire." Grainne spoke from the doorway. "How are you feeling?"

I am grave. Melancholy. Resolved. "I am well enough," Mhoire said, turning. She surveyed the muddy ground near her feet. "How long has it been raining?"

"All yesterday."

Mhoire looked toward the field still shrouded in darkness. "The rain will rot the seed."

Grainne touched her arm. "I know you are worried, Mhoire. But we can do well here. The rain will stop. You'll see."

"I can't go back to Ireland, Grainne."

"Nay."

"And I can't marry Drosten. He frightens me." She looked at her friend. "You understand, don't you?"

"Aye, I do."

"So we must protect ourselves."

"Aye." Grainne nodded emphatically.

"Will you carry a message for me? I can't go myself—Drosten's men have their eyes on me." She gestured toward the shadows.

Mhoire bent and whispered instructions in Grainne's ear. Then she pressed a small object into her friend's hand.

Chapter Thirteen

A sullen drizzle turned to a steady downpour that lasted all day. The wind came, too, in furious gusts that bent the grasses flat and lashed the green sea into frothy peaks.

Inside the gathering hall, everything was orderly. Buckets, pots, ladles, cups and bowls, which the Pictish warriors had brought with them and which had quietly become communal property, were stacked on planks of stone. Wattle shutters covered the windows and blocked the chill. Simple wooden benches, which the men had fashioned in their spare time, surrounded the central hearth. Rushlights slipped into iron pegs along the walls cast a golden domestic glow.

Still there was tension. After the rain had forced everyone inside, Mhoire fell to cleaning and tidying in complete silence, leaving the others to wonder if it was rage or despair that burdened her. Drosten wore an expression of such seriousness that even little Oran feared to approach him.

Toward evening, one of the sentries appeared on the threshold, his wet, dark hair like an inverted cup upon his head. Beside him stood an old man, half-bent at the waist and clutching a large package wrapped in leather.

He was as thin as a skeleton, and his long, ragged gown fell loosely from his narrow shoulders to his bony ankles. His beard stuck out in all directions, and his hair drifted about his head like dirty snow. The way he held himself, with his head tilted up and to the side, told Mhoire that he had spent his life listening, and that he was blind.

"It's rainin' cats and old wives out there, so when I saw him on the path I thought it best to bring him here for shelter," the sentry said as Mhoire and Drosten approached from opposite sides of the hall.

"It's the harper!" Brigit shouted. "Harper Neill!"

The old man smiled, and the folds of his skin pleated deeply. "That I am." He reached an arm out toward Mhoire. "And who is this?"

She grasped his hand. His fingers were cold as ice but strong. "I am Mhoire ni Colman, and this is Dun Darach."

"Dun Darach, aye. I meant to go to the chapel and beg a bit of food from the monks, but this fellow told me it was in ruins." His opaque blue eyes wandered in their sockets.

"Aye. And we are nearly so. But surely you do not travel alone, Harper Neill?"

"The fever stole my boy, two years' past."

Mhoire took in his threadbare clothes and his worn leather boots caked with mud. "How do you manage to survive?"

"Survive?" An impish smile played about the harper's mouth. "My dear, surviving is easy for me. You see, I can make magic." He patted the leather bundle he cradled in his arms. "And no one wants that to die."

The women sat Harper Neill down on one of the benches before the fire and immersed his feet in a bowl of warm water in which red moss had been boiled. Then they pressed a mug of birch-leaf tea—good for rheumatism— into his knobby hand.

A harper in the hall was a festive event, and excitement rang through the air. After supper was done, they cleared the floor around the hearth and gathered in a half-circle. Harper Neill unwrapped the leather covering from his harp and hoisted it, curved like the prow of a ship, upon his lap.

A few of the women sang. Harper Neill knew Pictish

songs, too, and when he played some of the faster, more raucous tunes, the men joined in, loudly. Drosten, Mhoire noticed, never sang, though his lips curved into a smile when his men bellowed with their greatest enthusiasm.

After half a dozen tunes, Fergus withdrew from inside his shirt a small pipe made of an eagle's bone.

"Do you know 'The Soldier's Lament'?" he asked Harper Neill.

The harper nodded, and the two began to play.

Mhoire would never have guessed red-haired Fergus, with his beefy hands and snaggled teeth, had such music in him. The sound of his pipe flowed through the air, as pure as a mountain stream. Each note was long and mournful, and spoke of loss and yearning, of hardship, and a life away from home.

The tune tore at Mhoire's heart. And then she looked at Drosten. He was staring, not at the piper nor the harper, but at something invisible between the two. The homeland he had left behind? The peaks of those glorious high mountains? The lush green fields he had tilled in his boyhood? The faces of his clan? In her mind's eye, Mhoire saw him among them, and for the first time she realized what he had given up by coming to the wreck that was Dun Darach. Everything he knew. Prosperity. Security. Rank. Comfort.

Drosten turned his head and caught her watching him. She saw the flicker of surprise on his face, but she could not look away, and for a moment her heart glowed in her eyes.

"Sing for us, Mhoire!"

She jumped. The song had come to a halt, and all eyes turned to her expectantly. A flush reddened her neck and face. "I don't—"

"Please!" little Oran piped up, clapping her hands. There was a rumble of assent.

The harper raised his hands to his strings. "How about 'The Story of the Snow-Child'? Do you know that one?"

"Well . . ." Mhoire looked around. She saw nothing but interest and anticipation on the circle of faces before her.

"Well, if you're sure you want it," she agreed reluctantly. "Just one verse."

She possessed a soft, sweet voice. It did not carry far, but held such emotion that everyone fell silent and stretched forward to hear it. When the harper carried on without interruption from the first verse to the second and then to the third, Mhoire, her cheeks flushed rosy as a robin's breast, stayed with him.

At Drosten she could bestow only glancing looks—fleeting sweeps through long lashes that were unconsciously coquettish. But he gazed at her, spellbound, with eyes that were warm and brilliant.

The look did not go unnoticed.

"We must do something about this," Elanta whispered, nudging Brigit with her elbow.

"Hmm." Brigit's eyes went from Mhoire to Drosten and back again. "Things seem to heat up between those two, but they never come to a boil."

"What can we do?"

"We could try ripping off their clothes and throwing them in the byre."

"Brigit! Be serious."

"Well, I'm half-serious. In truth, all it would take is to get them in close range and keep them there. I recognize the look that's burning in their eyes. Lust. Pure and simple."

Abruptly, Elanta stood. "Harper Neill!"

Fortunately, the tune was winding to a close, and its last few notes were cut only slightly short when the musician looked up in surprise.

"Play us a dance, Harper Neill!" Elanta shouted.

"A dance is it?" The women murmured their approval. The men shifted uneasily. Bawdy songs were great fun, but dancing? What soldier had opportunity to dance, except over his enemy's grave?

The harper launched into "The Fair-Haired Lass."

It was a ring dance for ladies only. Elanta and Brigit nudged the men off their seats and had them drag the benches against the walls to create an open space. They grabbed Mhoire between them, ignoring her feeble protests, and then all the women joined hands in a circle. Smiling, they moved to the right, and then to the left. On the second verse, they leapt lightly, seven times in one direction, seven times in the other, their gowns lifted high above their calves.

Watching closely for a glimpse of a well-turned leg or a bouncing breast, the men decided that dancing was not so horrible after all. So when Harper Neill dove into a sword dance, a few of the men were persuaded to attempt it. They leapt across their crossed weapons, grinning broadly and hair flying.

Still, Mhoire noticed, Drosten did not participate, though he threw his head back and laughed with the others at his soldiers' antics. When Harper Neill began to pluck out a couples' dance, and little Oran approached Drosten pleadingly, the Pictish leader tried to brush her off.

But Oran would not be dissuaded.

Drosten pointed to the cluster of men standing idle. With twenty men and only eight females present, there were plenty of extra partners. Oran shook her head vigorously. He crouched before her and began to speak with extreme patience. The child tugged on his arm till he almost toppled over. Finally, he sighed, rose, took her tiny hand, and let her pull him out to where the others had already begun to dance.

He was, indeed, clumsy. Mhoire had to cover her mouth with her hand to hide her amusement. It was a simple dance, and Oran's instructions were continuous. "Nay, nay! This way!" Mhoire heard her say. "Nay, nay! Move this foot now!" But Drosten's limbs seemed far too big for delicate movement.

No one had asked Mhoire to dance. At first she was relieved. Then she felt awkward. She was the only woman not on the dance floor. Even Nila was dancing. Mhoire had not thought herself to be so very offensive. At feasts and weddings, she had never wanted for partners. These men, she concluded, must believe her too peculiar to consort with. She stood alone against the wall and kept her eyes on the dancers to mask her discomfort. She did not realize that the soldiers shied from her pride and her beauty.

The next dance was unfamiliar, and she sighed and turned toward the door, thinking to step outside. She didn't see Elanta whisper in Oran's ear. Didn't see Oran command Drosten to remain where he was. Didn't notice the child skipping toward her until she was at her side, her face as red as an apple and her eyes bright.

"Mhoire! Dance with us!"

"I don't know this dance, Oran."

"I'll teach you!"

"I don't . . ."

"Come!" She dragged Mhoire to the spot where Drosten was standing.

He lifted an eyebrow in greeting.

Mhoire's nerves began to flutter. "But Drosten is your partner, Oran."

"It's a dance for three! Everybody hold hands!" She grabbed Drosten's hand while still clutching Mhoire's.

Drosten smiled a shy, crooked smile. "We're captives, *mo milidh*. I'll try not to break your toes." He took her hand in his.

He held it firmly as they moved forward together, and then back. Then they each took a turn dropping hands to go under the joined arms of the other two, a movement that caused Oran to launch into a fit of giggles as a very tall Drosten struggled to get under her and Mhoire's low arch. Then they made a small circle again, and Mhoire found herself welcoming the feel of Drosten's warm, calloused hand.

She glanced at his face and noticed the V of concentration between his brows. "You are doing very well," she noted.

He grinned. "At least I haven't hurt anyone yet."

The threesome moved to the right. "Didn't your ladylove teach you to dance?" she asked teasingly.

They shifted directions. Drosten stumbled slightly and recovered. "I can't say I've ever had a ladylove."

"What about your princess?"

Her question took him by surprise, and he stopped. She crashed into his side. He reached out and gripped her around the waist to keep her from falling. This time, thank God, she didn't scream. Instead, instinctively, her arms went to his shoulders. For a second they stood close, so close that her breasts grazed his chest and her legs pressed into his thighs, hard as tree trunks. He looked completely nonplussed by her words and she cursed herself for saying them.

But then his eyes warmed. "If Princess Fionna was my ladylove, then my horse is the angel Gabriel."

And then Oran pushed them into motion again. "Don't stop! Keep dancing!"

His words buoyed her. She didn't even notice the others' inquisitive looks, didn't care that her hair was coming loose and framing her face with damp curls, that her gown clung to the lush curves of her bottom, and that excitement plumped her lips and turned them the color of foxgloves. She only knew that when the harper stopped, Drosten kept her hand in his.

"Play 'Into the Woods, Lassie'!" Brigit called out.

"I don't know this one either," Mhoire murmured.

Drosten bent his head to hers. "Don't worry. Just follow Oran's instructions. Did I tell you I'm going to enlist her as my second in command?"

She laughed, and the music rang out once more—harp and pipe both this time—and the threesome joined hands. Mhoire did not know what she was in for. She was used to courtly dances with stately steps, not the wild gambols of the commoners. The tune was lively, and the onlookers stomped and clapped. At a crescendo, Oran shouted, "Pick me up!" and Drosten swung her high and around. And before Mhoire could even anticipate the next move, she was in his arms and he was lifting her off her feet and she was gliding like a bird in the air and looking down into his laughing eyes, and she smiled with the joy of it.

The truth hit her like an apple falling from a tree. God help her. She had fallen in love with him.

And then suddenly the music stopped, cut off as if it were sliced with a knife. Drosten set her back on her feet, and she saw Grainne at the door. Beside her stood Irwin, as thin as a crow and utterly expressionless.

Chapter Fourteen

The roar of the heavy sea and the wild skittering of the rain followed the visitors in through the door. Irwin had half a dozen men with him, all dripping water. Grainne followed behind them.

"Are you lost, Irwin, or just hungry?" Drosten called out.

"I sent for him," Mhoire said.

Drosten dropped his hold on her waist. "You? Why?"

"Because I need help building the wall."

He drew a breath but did not answer.

Irwin pointed limply toward the hearth. "I wouldn't mind taking a little warmth from that fire."

Mhoire stepped aside to let him pass.

The Pictish warriors moved off to one end of the hall—near the spot where their weapons were lying, Mhoire noted with slight alarm—and Irwin and his men gathered about the fire, where they sent out an odorous, wooly steam. Harper Neill rested his instrument on the floor by his side, clasped his hands over his thin belly, and pointed his nose alertly upwards, like an animal checking the air for interesting smells.

Drosten turned back to her.

"We have an agreement," he hissed. "You are to make your way alone here."

"We never said that I couldn't pay someone to help me."

"Pay?"

"Aye."

"What? What did you pay him?"

"A brooch."

"A *brooch*?"

"Aye. Of considerable value. It was my mother's."

"Your *mother's*?"

"Aye. He offered to help."

"Help?!"

"Why must you repeat everything I say? You're not a simpleton!"

Drosten's eyebrows shot up. "Nay, *mo milidh*, I'm not." He took a step closer. "You've given that fool a brooch, but I think you promised him something more. And I wager he thinks so, too."

Mhoire thanked Grainne for completing her mission and poured out hot water flavored with mint—all she could offer for drink—for Irwin and his men. She was looking over her small supply of grain and debating whether courtesy required her to make her guests oatcakes when the women surrounded her.

"Mhoire, what are you doing?" Brigit demanded.

Mhoire faced the group. Brigit's fists were on her hips, and her face was as ruddy as the strands of hair that hung about her face.

"We need Irwin's help. We must repair the wall."

"We have help," Elanta chimed in.

Mhoire turned to her. "I have explained all this before. I cannot ask the Picts for help. My task is to make Dun Darach prosper on my own. Then the Picts will leave here and return to their own country."

"But you asked Irwin," Elanta said.

"I have paid Irwin. I gave him a brooch."

"Hah!" Brigit snorted. "Men only know one kind of payment, and it's under a woman's skirt."

Mhoire blushed.

Elanta's eyes widened. "Mhoire, you're not planning on marrying Irwin, are you?"

Mhoire gathered her arguments. "It makes sense for me

to marry him. He is wealthy, he needs a wife, and he is a Scot. He's one of us."

The women said nothing.

"You are the ones who brought him to my attention."

"Aye, but only as a contrast," Elanta said woefully. "We never thought you'd choose him for a husband. What about Drosten? He's big and strong. And he wants you!"

Mhoire closed her eyes. How could she make them understand that Drosten was too big, too strong? He would overwhelm her, like a sea that lifts and breaks. It would drag her into its vastness. And it would drown her. She had lived most of her life feeling frightened and helpless, and she could not bear those emotions any longer.

"Listen to me. You know I don't particularly want to marry anyone. I wish we had a stout fort and fields overflowing with grain. But we don't. We have nothing. You saw my father. Do you think he will leave us be to peacefully plant posies? We're not safe here by ourselves. I can't jeopardize your lives as well as my own. And Irwin would be quiet. We'd hardly know he was around, not like—" She bit her lip.

More silence.

She tried another tactic. "Look. Irwin has many fine men under his command." She gestured toward the cluster around the fire, but none of the women so much as turned a head. "They're quite good-looking. I instructed Grainne to ask Irwin to bring handsome ones."

"You what?" That was Brigit, outraged. "What do you think we are? Horses to be traded?"

"Nay, Brigit! But you said you wanted husbands. I only thought to arrange for some. Now look—" She took Brigit by the shoulders and turned her to face Irwin's soldiers. "See how attractive they are? Their tunics are clean, and their hair is cut, and their weapons—see how fine their weapons are? Look at that dark-haired one there, Brigit, talking to Irwin, or that bearded fellow next to him. The one who's warming his hands."

Brigit made a face.

Mhoire turned her toward the Picts, who were huddled in twos and threes, scowling. "Now look at these men. They're . . . they're scruffy. And their clothing is just . . . hanging about them. You can tell they don't care anything about their appearance. And their hair needs trimming. It's way too long and wild looking. And those . . . those designs they have pierced on their arms and legs. It's like they put them there just to show off their big muscles. They're . . . they're . . ."

"Masculine," Brigit said with an emphatic nod. "Good brawny men. We like them."

The other women nodded their agreement.

"But you can't," Mhoire said limply.

"But we do," Brigit answered, turning to face her. "We've already made our choices, and not for any lily-faced boys like those ones over there." She bobbed her head toward Irwin's soldiers.

"But the Picts are your longtime enemies, and Irwin's men are our friends."

"Friends is as friends does," Brigit said. "And true friends don't have to be paid."

"You have a very nice hall here." Mhoire and Irwin stood next to the hearth. The others had moved a little distance away. Except, that is, for Drosten. As soon as Mhoire had approached Irwin, he had rooted himself, uninvited, at her side.

"Thank you. It's very spacious," she noted, surveying the bare walls. She glanced at Drosten. He had his arms folded across his chest and was frowning at the ground.

"Have you had an accident?"

Mhoire turned to Irwin with a puzzled brow. He was staring at the bruises on her face.

"It's none of your affair," Drosten growled.

There was an awkward silence.

Mhoire scanned the room. Everyone was eyeing everyone else. Men looking at men, men looking at women,

women looking at men—the undercurrent of turbulence was enough to make her seasick.

"Would you care for a stroll around the room?" Irwin asked.

"As you wish." A stroll seemed innocent enough.

She took a few steps away from the fire, with Irwin at her right elbow.

Drosten fell in on her other side.

"I don't need a chaperone," she whispered loudly.

Drosten clasped his hands behind his back.

The triumvirate reached a corner and turned.

"You know, Drosten," Mhoire said, surveying the hall, "I think you might want to go over there and say a word to your men."

"Why?"

"Because I see a fight about to break out."

Drosten raised his eyes. Some of his soldiers had joined Irwin's contingent and were talking loudly. He shrugged.

Stubborn!

They continued walking.

Mhoire cleared her throat. "I appreciate your assistance with the wall, Irwin."

"Happy to help a fellow countryman . . . er . . . woman."

"You've been to Dun Darach before?"

"Of course."

"And did you watch it burn?" Drosten interjected, casting a sudden ferocious look over Mhoire's head.

Irwin hesitated. "I had no choice. If my men had joined the battle, they would have been slaughtered. There was nothing I could do to save the fort."

They turned another corner.

"I can only work on the wall tomorrow," Irwin said abruptly. "Then I must return home and take the men with me."

"I see." Mhoire frowned. For a brooch, she had expected more.

"It's because of the Britons. I can't be away for long."

"What about the Britons?" Drosten asked.

"They're on the move. They've been spotted east of here."

"And what do they want?" Mhoire asked, her brow furrowing.

"What everyone wants," Drosten answered. "Land. Especially land along the coast, like this island. Dun Darach has a view of the sea lanes. Whoever controls the sea lanes controls the entire countryside."

"So Dun Darach's location gives it value, regardless of what the fields yield," Mhoire mused. "More value than most holdings." She turned toward Irwin. "More value even than your land."

"Perhaps." Irwin watched her with watery eyes.

"This is all about power, Mhoire," Drosten said. "With the Danes closing in, only the powerful will survive."

"And the rest of us?"

No one spoke.

Chapter Fifteen

Harper Neill shuffled off the next morning. Drosten left soon after. Off to check on the whereabouts of the Britons, he told Mhoire. Alone, so as not to leave Dun Darach short of soldiers and more vulnerable than it already was. He ordered his men to help repair the wall. "I won't see you—or anyone else—killed in my presence," he flung over his shoulder to Mhoire as he mounted his horse. "Agreement or no."

And still it rained. Mizzle changed to shower changed to mist. Water streamed off the cliffs and plunged into the fields, transforming them into great muddy puddles. Every able person worked on the wall until their hands stiffened into claws.

Irwin left at nightfall and took his men with him. Soaked to the bone, Mhoire changed into another gown, dark blue, with a low, fitted bodice and tight sleeves. She unbound her hair and let it fall loose past her shoulders to dry. Why should she care about the seemliness of her appearance? All these men wanted from her was her land. If they didn't care about her, she wouldn't care about them. She wouldn't care that Drosten had been gone all day. Wouldn't care that the weather was roiling. Wouldn't care that the sentries had seen no sign of him.

But when he appeared at the door, her heart lurched in her chest. His hair was plastered to his head, and his eyes were half-focused. She could tell by the way he clutched at the doorpost that something was wrong.

She stood. "What is it?"

He shook his head like a dog, and beads of water flew off his hair. "It's naught to do with you."

He was pale as a corpse.

"You're hurt."

He dropped his hand from the doorpost, straightened, and swayed on his heels. "I'm fine."

"Come in and sit down."

"I'm not a mouse like your new friend Irwin. I don't need to sit down."

Her eyes traveled the length of him and settled on the pool of water at his feet. The pool that was turning red. "Drosten, you are dripping blood all over the floor. If you don't come in and sit down, I will go over there and push you down."

He closed his eyes a moment and reached for the doorpost again. "I would very much like to see you try, *mo milidh*—" And his legs began to buckle.

Brian and Alfred reached him before he hit the floor. They dragged him to the fire.

"Take those wet clothes off him," Mhoire commanded. "Grainne, get some blankets."

She averted her eyes while the men stripped him. "Look for his wounds, and tell me where they are."

"Left arm's a bloody mess," Brian said. "Cuts across the chest."

"Turn him over. Check the other side."

She heard a groan.

"Back's clean. More cuts on the legs. But the arm's the worst of it."

"All right." Mhoire turned and cast her eyes over the damage. Drosten's left arm was streaked with blood and sweat. She peered more closely. The wound itself was above the elbow, about two inches long and very deep. She probed the edges, and Drosten opened his eyes.

"Who stabbed you?" she asked. "And don't tell me you

fell off your horse because I know a stab wound when I see it."

He raised his head a fraction and peered at the cut. "It's not bad. Leave it be."

"Grainne," she called over her shoulder. "Bring me my bag of medicines, hot water, and clean rags." She turned back and pulled the blanket down to Drosten's waist. The cuts on his chest were superficial. They could wait. She tucked the blanket up around his torso, leaving the wounded arm exposed. "Just lie there. I need to sew this up."

Grainne returned with the herbs and Elanta carried the water. "There are no rags," Grainne announced. "There's no cloth to spare. We used it all for bedding."

"Tear up my night shift."

Drosten groaned. "I don't want your night shift."

She looked up at Brian and Alfred. "Do you have anything strong to give him to drink?"

"Ah, you don't want Drosten drinking, lady," Brian answered.

"Whyever not?"

The men exchanged looks. "He's not much of a drinker," Alfred explained. "So when he does drink, he gets, uh . . . peculiar."

"Peculiar?" Mhoire wrinkled her brow. "What does he do? Stand on his head and sing?"

The men exchanged another look.

"Get the drink, Brian, and if he gets rowdy, you'll have to hold him down for me. Or I'll sit on him."

Brian grinned and went for the flask.

A big, thirsty man can hold a lot of fluid, and the whiskey flowed easily down Drosten's throat. As she waited for its pain-numbing effects to take hold, Mhoire sponged the blood off his arm and bound a compress against the wound to stop the flow. Then she cleaned the small cuts on his chest and his thighs. He was docile now—half-asleep, she hoped. She tried not to notice how magnificent he was, how his muscles and sinews wrapped compactly around his bones, how straight his limbs were, how firm his trunk under the soft, tawny hair that covered his chest. Her hands traveled over him, padding him here and there, and he shivered under her touch. She felt his forehead, fearing fever, but it was cool. Then she cupped her hands under his head, and he opened his eyes.

"Are you trying to put me back together or tear me apart, *mo milidh*?" he murmured drowsily.

"I was feeling for breaks in the bones. Now here—" Her fingers gently probed his scalp and found a lump the size of a walnut. "I thought I'd find this. You were hit on the head, weren't you?" She looked down into his indigo eyes. They were amused.

"How did you know that?"

"Because you look so stupid."

He closed his eyes and smiled. "More stupid than us'al, you mean?"

His words were slurred. Good. She leaned back and picked up her needle. "Was it the Britons?"

"Don't know. Forgot to ask where they came from."

"Are they dead?"

He shook his head. "Nay, more's the pity." He yawned. "Just damaged them enough that they ran away."

"You shouldn't travel alone."

He opened one eye and watched her thread the needle. "I've had one battle today, *mo milidh*. Let's not have another."

The others gathered round as she made the first stitch. She looked up to see how Drosten had taken it.

He was staring at her with dark, melting eyes.

"Does this hurt?" she asked. "Would you like more whiskey?"

"Don't need it," he murmured. "It's you who makes me drunk."

She stilled, her hand with the needle mid-air. She glanced at Alfred, who raised an eyebrow.

She took another stitch.

"Like that gown."

She stilled again, and saw where his eyes had traveled. To her neckline, and the swell of her breasts, amply revealed as she crouched over him. "Keep your eyes closed. You'll feel less pain."

"Umm. And less pleasure."

She heard smothered giggles behind her. She bit her lip and took a few more stitches.

Each stitch brought her face closer to his.

"You're beautiful," he whispered.

"Drosten, you are drunk."

"I told you—"

"I know. I make you drunk." She leaned back to get more thread and heard a muffled laugh. She glanced up at Brian and Alfred, who quickly composed their faces and shrugged their shoulders.

She threaded the needle and bent over Drosten once more. He was quiet for a while and let her concentrate on her work, though his eyes never left her face. She stitched as carefully and as quickly as she could. The skin around the wound was red and inflamed, and each prick of her needle must have felt like a hot iron. But he didn't flinch.

"Why's your hair down?" he murmured.

"It got wet today. I'm letting it dry."

"It's like a cloud. Lovely . . . dark . . . cloud."

She struggled to keep her voice light. "I didn't know you were a poet."

"Me neither." He lifted his right hand and touched a lock that was falling across her shoulder.

She didn't know what to make of him.

"I'll steep some willow tea to ease the pain."

He shook his head. "It's you who hurt me, *mo milidh*," he said, fingering her hair.

She bit her lip. "I know. The needle hurts."

"Not the needle."

She took a breath. Avoiding his eyes, she bent again to her task.

"Don't marry him."

"Who?"

"You know who. Irwin, the mouse."

She slipped the needle into the skin. "I didn't say I was going to marry him."

"You're thinking of it."

She didn't answer.

"He can't appreciate you. Doesn't know how."

She pinched the top of the wound together and made the last stitch. "You and I weren't going to fight, remember?"

"Don't want to fight with you, *mo milidh*. Ever."

She cut the thread with her dagger and tied a knot. "Why do you call me that? *Mo milidh*—'my warrior'?"

He smiled. "Because that's what you are. The best kind." He fingered a dark tendril. "Full of passion. Courage."

She lowered her head. "Not courage."

His next words were so low she almost didn't hear them. "Kiss me, *mo milidh*."

Chapter Sixteen

Drosten's pupils were dark, almost black.

"Drosten—"

"Kiss me."

Behind her, the others shuffled away.

She lowered her head. "Nay," she whispered. "You're daft."

"I promise I won't pounce. Too besotted."

Her heart thumped. Then she lowered her head and grazed his lips with hers. Near-blind with embarrassment, she groped for her bag. Drawing it onto her lap, she fumbled within it. "I must make a . . . a poultice for the wound."

When she dared steal a look at his face, he was asleep.

"I didn't."

"You did."

"I kissed her?" Drosten's mouth dropped open. It was mid-morning. He had awakened a few minutes earlier to an empty hall and an aching arm, and Grainne, poking him in the ribs and insisting he sit up so she could inspect his wound. Now she was peeling away the bandage, and none too carefully.

"In truth, you made *her* kiss *you*."

He peered into the woman's face. "You are inventing this tale."

Grainne peered back. "Why, in the name of Mary and Joseph and all the saints, would I want to do that?"

Drosten lifted his shoulders in a mighty shrug. "I . . . have no idea."

Grainne probed the wound lightly, her lips pursed. "I don't tell tales."

"Then tell me this—"

"Don't raise your voice to me. You're not my clansman."

He lowered his voice. "Tell me this. How, when I can't get that woman to do a single other thing that I ask, could I get her to kiss me?"

"You were drunk."

That shut him up. Truth be told, his head was pounding. It was like he had a cathedral full of bells inside it.

"And you begged."

Begged? Could he have gotten *that* drunk? "I never beg."

"You did last night."

He blinked a few times. Then he cleared his throat. "What did I say?"

Grainne sniffed his wound. "No pus. You're lucky." She reached for a small wooden bowl. "You told her she was beautiful and courageous."

A flush stole up Drosten's neck. "She is beautiful and courageous."

"Aye." Grainne pounded the concoction inside the bowl with a wooden pestle. "And she doesn't need the likes of you playing tricks on her and trying to lead her down a path she doesn't want to go."

"Tricks!"

"Shh. Stop bellowing."

"There's no one here, woman! And I'm not bellowing!"

Grainne squinted at him. "And I suppose you weren't using one of your warrior strategems on her last night, either."

Drosten filled his cheeks and exploded a breath. "How could I use strategems when I was drunk!"

"So—" Grainne scooped out two fingers full of a yellow-brown substance from her bowl and dabbed it on Drosten's arm. "—so you wanted to kiss her for herself alone."

He didn't answer.

She looked up at him, eyes narrowed.

"Well—" He cleared his throat again. "She's very beautiful."

"You said that." She spread the substance over the wound.

Drosten wrinkled his nose. "What is this stuff?"

"Yarrow. And a little cow urine. Draws out the poisons."

He frowned and watched her work for a moment. "She is supposed to be my wife, you remember."

"Hah!" Grainne dug into the bowl for another dollop of poultice.

Drosten shifted his position, searching for a more comfortable spot on the ground. Not only was his head agitated, his entire body seemed to be in an uproar. He rubbed the back of his neck.

"So, er—" he said. "—she, er, she kissed me then?"

"You don't remember?"

"Nay, I, er . . . don't."

"Aye, she kissed you. For a long time, too."

Damnation! How could he not remember that? "And then what did I do?"

"Started snoring."

Drosten's mouth dropped again. "You mean we kissed and I fell asleep?"

Grainne nodded. "Out like a candle."

"I wouldn't have."

"Oh, but you did. From what I hear, that's what men always do."

She reached for more of the poultice and rubbed it in.

"Did she kiss Irwin too?"

"Not yet."

"Not yet!"

"Must you be so loud?"

"I am not loud. I am perfectly calm." He composed his face for a moment. Then he threw up his hands. "And you talk about *my* strategems! What about her feminine wiles? What about the way she's . . . she's *seducing* Irwin with her hairpins and brooches and smiles?"

"Mhoire doesn't know a feminine wile from a billygoat." Grainne reached for a piece of white linen. "All she is trying to do is protect the people who live here. I brought the brooch to Irwin, as payment for his help repairing the wall, and that's all that was paid. There's been no promise made to him about marriage. Not even a discussion as near as I can tell. But who could blame her if she did marry him? She needs help and she's doing what she can to get it."

"So why did she kiss me? Is she trying to soften me up so I take pity on her?"

"More likely she took pity on you."

"I don't need her pity."

"I agree with that." Grainne tore off a length of the linen.

Drosten rubbed his face with his hand. His skin felt like it was stuck to his bones. "So . . . would she actually give herself in marriage to this idiot?"

Grainne narrowed her eyes. "Are you jealous?"

"Why should I be jealous?"

The woman shook her head silently and began to wrap the cloth around his arm.

"Just because a pretty woman goes chasing after another man, it doesn't mean it has to affect me."

"Un-huh."

"You know she's not even the right kind of woman for me."

Grainne wound the bandage once around again.

"I need a woman who is . . . who is . . . ." He raked his hand through his hair. "Well, I can't think of what I need. But it's not a woman who's always trotting around, giving brooches to strange men, buying cows, and . . . and . . . arguing with me all the time."

Grainne tore off another piece of cloth.

"And," Drosten continued, warming to his subject, "I'm clearly the wrong man for her. Clearly, she likes mousy types of men, who simper around showing off their fine clothes and elegant manners." He nodded his head emphatically. "So we'd be miserable with each other. It doesn't matter that I want to kiss her. It's just curiosity. And that's likely why she kissed me. Like kissing a porcupine or something. Just to see what it's like."

"A porcupine—" A snort burst through Grainne's nose. She glanced at his hair, which was standing on end. "Well, I do see some resemblance." She tied a knot in the bandage. Then she gave him a level gaze. "So why marry her, if you are so unsuited?"

"Because I must. And what does it matter how we're suited? That's not the point of marriage."

"But you care for her nonetheless."

"I . . . I'm concerned about her."

"How, then, can you deny her her future?"

He flushed. "It's my future too. My country's future. Our safety." He leaned toward her. "My mother died because of the Danes. I cannot stand by and see more women struck down. Not my countrywomen. Not Mhoire. Not you. My family did not make this marriage contract to thwart her plans, to ruin her life. It has nothing to do with her."

"It has everything to do with her. A woman is not a thing to be traded, no matter what law and custom say." Grainne tapped his bandage. "See this? This is Mhoire's night shift, I'll have you know. She tore it to pieces to keep you from bleeding to death, and you don't even remember."

Drosten's eyes hardened. "What is it you hold against me, woman? What evil have I done?"

"You're standing in her way. You want to keep her from being herself. And she's never been herself. Always she's had to hide from her father, not disturb her mother, make herself invisible. She deserves a chance to discover who she is and what she wants."

"And she wants poverty and danger and, no doubt, a speedy death, living alone with these women and this falling-to-pieces fort?"

"There is the other alternative."

"Irwin again. Irwin is the alternative. And you think—
she thinks—she can live a good life with him?"

Grainne shrugged.

Lord, he felt like his head was going to blow into pieces.
"Irwin," he went on, "is the one who can't be trusted. He
doesn't truly want her. Not for herself."

Grainne gathered up her bowl and spoon, as if she hadn't
heard him.

"Why does she choose him and not me?" he persisted,
as Grainne lifted herself to her feet.

She looked down at him sharply. "Because you want her
too much."

Mhoire was mortified. And exhilarated. And clumsy.

Every item she picked up that morning—her boot, her
bowl, her shawl—seemed to fall out of her hands of its
own accord. Or maybe it was because her hands were so
very unsteady. As was her heart.

She had blushed when Elanta spooned out her porridge.
Blushed again when one of the men mentioned Drosten's
name. Nearly choked when Brigit joked about "the sorry
state of a man in drink." Finally, she had bolted into the
courtyard without allowing herself more than the tiniest of
glances at the large, quiescent form sleeping near the hearth
that was causing so much turbulence.

She grabbed the wooden bucket that sat by the door and
strode toward the gate, thinking to fetch water from the
spring. *What did it mean—that kiss? Did he truly desire
her?* A man deep in ale could say all sorts of unexpected
things, but his tongue was usually loosened to the truth,
not tied up in deception.

You are beautiful, Drosten had said. *Passionate.* She
clung to the words as she clung to her shawl.

She slipped through the gateway and stopped. She
needed to think. She needed privacy. Instead of heading
down to the spring, she turned right and skirted the outside
of the wall. After a dozen paces, she tucked herself into a
spot where the wall was high enough to keep her out of

sight of the sentries and other curious eyes. She leaned back against the cool stones and looked toward the loch.

She closed her eyes, and immediately, her mouth recalled the touch of Drosten's lips. How pliant they were, yet firm. Responsive and sweet. Patient and enticing. She imagined pressing up against him. Feeling all of him—his chest and his thighs and his shoulders. And his warm lips, traveling over her brow and her cheeks and her throat.

"He was fooling."

Mhoire's eyes snapped open.

"You think so?"

The voices came from the other side of the wall. Two of Drosten's soldiers.

"What else? You know Drosten. He's got a silver tongue when it comes to getting what he wants out of people."

"Aye. When it's a soldier afeared to march into his first battle. But a woman now? He's never had much to do with them."

"Och. It's all the same. Canny, he is."

"Aye. I'll give him that."

"Got her, too, didn't he?"

The men laughed, their voices fading as they walked away.

Mhoire's chest tightened, and for a moment she didn't think she could breathe. Then the muscle of her heart knotted and hardened and shrunk till it was nothing but a pebble rattling around in her chest.

She heard voices on the hillside below her—men coming to work on the wall. Panicking—*Please, God, don't let anyone see me now!*—she scrambled, head down, back toward the path to the spring, bucket knocking against her knees.

Near-frozen with shock and blind with hurt, she nearly ran into him.

He had come looking for her, needing to test the truth of Grainne's words. Was it possible to kiss a woman and not remember it?

One look at Mhoire's scarlet face told Drosten that it was.

He felt as awkward as a two-year-old.

He was blocking her way, and so she stopped. But it was not lost on him that she did not care to.

"You are fetching water?" he asked, nodding at her bucket. *Stupid question.*

She didn't answer but stared at something past his shoulder, her face set, her flaming skin the only sign of emotion.

He burned with remorse. What had it cost her to kiss him? To touch a man, and a drunken one at that? Lord in heaven, how could he have asked it of her?

Because he longed for her, longed for her now, for the softness that he knew was there, underneath the shell she wore to keep her fears at bay.

"I'll help you," he said, reaching out.

She scrambled back a step and slipped on the scree that littered the path. "Nay. I can do it."

He stood silently, struck dumb by her rejection.

She glanced at him and looked away. "How is your arm?"

He looked at his arm, as if he had forgotten it was there. "It's fine."

"You think the Britons attacked you?"

"Who else? Though they were fools to come after me. Now we know they're near. We can prepare."

She nodded, her eyes still fixed on some far point.

"Mhoire, I'm sorry."

A line appeared between her brows. Deepened. Her lips pressed together. She was crumpling now, her fragile shell collapsing, the shards of it turning inwards and tearing as they fell.

"You humiliated me!" Her words were strangled. Anger was fighting to get out and find him, and cause him pain.

For her sake, he let it. "I know."

"In front of all those people!"

"I know. I was wrong."

"You think I'm a silly maid? You think one kiss will win me over and then you can do what you will with me?"

"Nay, Mhoire. Nothing like that."

The gulls set off a clamorous cry. They had found a school of fish.

"I will not be dallied with." Her body was shaking now. Her emotions knocked against her bones in a way he had come to know, in a way he knew frightened her. He said the only thing he thought he could to calm her.

"I will never ask you to touch me again, Mhoire. If I should, you need not respond."

He didn't know the damage that he caused.

Chapter Seventeen

The nightmare is always the same. His mother is kneeling. A man crouches over her, like a panther. Only the man's hair is yellow-red, and a bronze serpent coils around his arm, and the serpent's head is raised and ready to strike. And the man's hands are around his mother's throat.

Her face is gray, still, as if she were already dead.

His sister is screaming. Two of the yellow men grip her thrashing body between them. She is a wild thing, a banshee of terror, howling for her mother.

No one touches him. His ears ring from the blow they have given him. His mouth is filled with blood, more bitter than bile. He can barely see, the pain a tunnel he must peer through. The men are asking him a question. They ask the same question over and over. And whenever he tries to answer, blood spurts from his mouth. He tries harder and harder to hurl out the words, until the ground is scarlet-red and his mother's face fades. And still his sister's screams rattle in his ears.

Drosten jolted awake, drenched in sweat. Then he realized that the crazed sound he was hearing was not his lost sister's cry, but horses whinnying with fear.

He knew the sounds of battle in his bones, and instinctively, he grabbed his sword and his axe and leapt to his feet. He headed toward the commotion at a dead run.

"Mhoire!" he shouted, as he reached the door of the gathering hall.

"I'm here! What is it?"

"Stay inside!" he yelled into the darkness. "Gather the women. Keep everyone inside." In rapid Pictish, he brought his men to arms.

The courtyard was in chaos. Men were swarming over the wall, and Drosten saw his sentries fall. "Stay together! Defend the hall!" he shouted. It was too late to secure the fort.

He looked to the water for a slim ship with a dragon's prow and square sails, but saw none.

Two men hurtled toward him. He pierced one with his sword, and warm blood splattered his face. He felled the other with a heavy axe blow that cleaved the man's shoulder, sundering muscle from bone.

Other foes replaced them, and Drosten heaved his weapons against them. His killing was methodical, emotionless, as it was in every battle.

They were outnumbered, and he sensed his soldiers struggling. They hurled no victory yells, no fiercesome battle cries. One man may battle two or three, but for each to fight off four at once would take a miracle.

Drosten shouted for his men to regroup around him, but they were too engaged in fighting for their own lives to hear. And then he was surrounded—five men, axes held high, mouths gaping open.

The first one lunged. Drosten knocked away his sword, then skewered him in the gut. He fought off the second with the hilt of his axe, even as he pulled his sword from the first. A third man came at his right, and Drosten lashed out again with his sword, slicing his enemy across the hand and setting off a yowling that made the others even more furious.

Two hurtled toward him at once. He beat them back. But there were two others now, behind him. Dread cloaked Drosten like Satan's black wings, and he braced himself for a death blow.

Suddenly, a man screamed. Drosten turned and saw him fall face down into the mud, like a tree in a storm. Then the other stiffened, his mouth a startled O, and crumpled beside his comrade. Swiftly, Drosten faced forward again, but his attackers were running toward the gate. So were others—to the gate, over the wall—and his warriors were chasing them. Panting, Drosten scanned the courtyard. It was littered with bodies. And most of them had an arrow in their back.

An arrow.

Fear—the fear that Drosten's dream would not release— filled his throat again. Someone, who should have been safe inside the hall, had been out amidst the terror shooting arrows. He ran, each breath a knifethrust to his chest, looking for the archer. He found her at the base of the wall, face down in the mud, motionless, her long, curving bow clutched in her hand.

Chapter Eighteen

Drosten and Alfred carried Mhoire into the hall. Her pulse was rapid and weak, and her breath as shallow as a fledgling bird's.

With her bow and quiver, she had positioned herself on the wall. It had given her the best vantage point for shooting, but had made her an easy target. An enemy arrow had found her there, after she had felled nearly a dozen men, turned the tide of the battle, and saved them all.

The arrow had pierced her left shoulder just above the heart and was lodged there still.

But it must come out.

Drosten swallowed hard. He had taken out many an arrow on the battlefield, but never had his palms sweated so. He wiped his hands on his tunic. "Let's lift her up." Alfred took Mhoire's weight on one side. Grainne, tears streaming down her face, braced her friend on the other.

She whimpered as Drosten tugged the arrow out, but her eyes stayed closed. God was kind and had taken her past feeling.

Nila laid a poultice of plaintain against Mhoire's shoulder. Then she took a strand of linen from what was left of Mhoire's nightshift and wrapped it tight around her torso.

"We must lay her down by the fire," Nila said. "Can you carry her, Drosten?"

Nodding, he gathered Mhoire close with one arm and slipped the other under her knees. He rose to his feet. She felt like a kitten in his arms. But her body held no animation, and her face was deathly pale.

"What can you give her for the pain?" he asked, as he lowered Mhoire onto a heather mattress. "Valerian?"

"She is past that, Drosten," Nila said.

He looked up, brow furrowed. "But she will need it when she rouses. We should have it ready."

Nila put a hand on Drosten's shoulder. "This is a grievous wound."

He turned back to Mhoire and watched as Elanta drew a blanket up to her chin. "I have seen worse. I have had worse."

Nila and Elanta exchanged glances. "I have no doubt," Nila said gently.

Drosten let Nila bathe his own wound, which had opened in the fighting, and stitch him up again. But exhausted as he was, he would not rest. He saw graves dug for two of his men and examined the others' injuries. He stationed those who were least hurt on the wall and sent four men to the woods to fell trees for a stockade. Whoever had attacked them would likely come again, and they must raise a higher defense.

Finally, when he had done what he could to protect the fort, he drew off his filthy clothes, poured a bucket of water over his head, and pulled on a clean linen shirt and tunic. His entire body trembled now, and it was taking all of the energy he had left to keep it under control. Pale and silent, he walked back into the quiet hall, sat down next to Mhoire, and buried his face in his knees.

He prayed. First in Latin, as the priests had taught him. Then in Gaelic, which he had learned at his mother's knee. And finally, in Pictish, the tongue he was born to and the language of his heart.

The fever came in the evening. Unquenchable, consuming. Helpless in the sea of heat, Mhoire rose and sank, in and out of consciousness.

She was hot, hotter than she had ever been, hotter than she thought a person could be.

The pain in her chest was a different kind of heat, a fiery knife that plunged deep into her body. It hurt to move. It hurt to breathe. But her body wouldn't stop breathing. And every breath was a sob.

Her tears lay cold upon her face and offered no relief. They ran down her chin and puddled damply on her pillow.

She was alone. So alone. Alone in the sea of heat and relentless pain. Alone when the death dreams came.

First, the *sluagh* from the fairy hill. Dark, slithering shapes that swirled around her like a flock of crows, noisy and black.

Then Colman. *Nay! Nay!* She struggled to run, and pain flashed white like lightning.

Grainne. Worried. Sad. Her friend. Grainne's voice, steady and true. Near, but far.

Mother. *Mother!* She reached out. *Mother!* Eveline stood at the foot of her bed. Watched silently. Melted away.

Faces. Darkness. Death.

Dying brought memories, and she was too weak to chase them away. They came like waves breaking against the shore, one upon another. Dark rooms. Loud voices. Crying.

Secrets.

A still body, lying on a velvet coverlet. The body that bore her.

And just when she thought that the memories would tear her apart, leave her broken like a rock under the sea, death came. And death was an angel. It stood in the house of her soul, drew its sword, and chased the spectres away. Then it folded its wings and watched over her with sober, gentle eyes.

Death gave her time to think.

What had she done with her life? *So little.*

What could she have done with her life, if she had kept on living? She ached over the loss and sobbed with self-pity.

Was she ready to die? *Nay, sweet Mary, nay.*

But death was here.
She must be ready.
She must think of what was important.
She must make things right.

They gave her dandelion water, wringing it from a cloth and dripping it slowly into a corner of her mouth. And then wormwood, ten draughts. But still the fever raged.

Drosten sat by her side in an agony of frustration as she whimpered and sobbed. She grew wild, and he held her down while Grainne wiped her cheeks with a cloth. Once Mhoire gripped his arm with shocking strength and half-raised herself from her bed. She cried out for her mother, a wrenching, heart-rending cry. Nila bent close and laid a hand upon her face, and Mhoire fell back, motionless.

Grainne sobbed then, deep, suffocating gulps. Alfred dropped down beside her and took her hand.

Mhoire's wounds broke open. They sponged her, front and back. Nila made a paste of yarrow—Achilles' magic herb. She chanted the ancient incantation: "May she be an isle in the sea. May she be a hill upon the shore. May she be a star at the waning of the moon."

For a while she quieted. Then she began to weep again, like an injured animal. Finally, Nila made a concoction of St. John's wort, the demon-chaser, the Virgin Mary's plant. Drosten held Mhoire up while they coaxed it into her mouth, and at last, she slept.

He must have dozed himself, for he woke to the feel of her eyes upon his face. They were dark as a winter cloud, serious, and intent. Her lips were blue. She whispered something, and he bent close.

"A priest," she said, the words barely audible.

"Nay," he countered, shaking his head, not wanting the death sacrament to fall between them, to take her farther away. "You are better. You will get well now."

Tears welled in her eyes, and she reached for him. He found her hand and clasped it. "Please. Marry me."

His breath caught in his throat. "Marry you?"

"Please. The women. They need a protector. Please."

"Mhoire, I—"

"Please." She gripped his hand with the little strength she had left, and tears spilled down her cheeks. "I have done such a terrible thing—"

"Nay—"

"I have thought only of myself. They will all die here alone. But you will protect them. I know you will."

He could only stare at her. Coldness ate at his gut, like acid.

"Please, Drosten. You want Dun Darach. You need it for your people." She was straining now, and sweat dripped from her forehead. "If you marry me, it will be yours when I die. You'll take care of the women, won't you? And the child?"

"I don't want it to be like this. I never wanted it to be like this." His hand tightened around hers.

"Promise me you'll take care of them." Her voice fell low, but her eyes clung to his.

The muscles in his throat convulsed. "Mhoire—"

"Please."

Her hand lay cold in his palm. "Aye. As you wish. I promise," he said.

From somewhere deep inside, she pulled out a glimmer of a smile.

"Doth thou take this woman?"

"Aye."

"Doth thou take this man?"

"Aye."

To have. To hold. From this day forward. From life into death.

From the depths have I cried to thee, O Lord; Lord, hear my voice. Let thine ears be attentive to the voice of my petition. For with thee there is merciful for-giveness. My soul hath relied on His word; my soul hath hoped in the Lord. From the morning watch even until night, I hath hoped in the Lord. Because with the Lord there is mercy, and with Him plentiful redemption.

Misereatur vestri omnipotens Deus, et dimissis peccatis vestris, perducat vos ad vitam aeternam.

Amen.

Chapter Nineteen

On the third day, Mhoire opened her eyes, shivering uncontrollably and as cold as snow. With trembling hands, she pulled the blanket a fraction closer to her chin.

Her movements caught Grainne's attention, and her friend's warm, dry hand fell on her forehead. "The fever's gone," Grainne said.

Others gathered.

"She's soaked."

"And the bedding as well."

"We must get her into something dry."

"But what? Her own things are torn to shreds, and the only spare shift among us is the one she's wearing now."

"I have something," a man's deep voice said. Awkwardly, Drosten held out a heavy piece of cloth. "Will this do?"

It was a long tunic of fine wool, the color of primroses.

Hands lifted Mhoire to a sitting position on the bed. Pain flashed in her chest, and the room went white. Unwillingly, she cried out.

The women pulled off Mhoire's sodden shift and dropped Drosten's tunic over her head. It was voluminous. The shoulders fell halfway to her elbows, and the sleeves covered her hands. But the material was soft against her skin.

She felt as limp as a piece of string, unable to sit upright on her own, and her mind was wrapped in cobwebs, as if it had been kept in an old cellar too long.

"We must dry out this bedding."

"Aye. It's wet as a puddle. Drosten!" Elanta called quietly. "Come and hold her for us."

He gathered her into his arms, mindful of her wounded left side. He felt as solid as a ship on the sea. She buried her cold nose in his shoulder and felt the warmth of him reach into her bones.

Holding her against his chest, Drosten leaned back against the wall. He pulled the collar of the tunic high around her neck and tucked the hem around her bare feet. Someone dropped a blanket over the both of them.

"Are you warm enough?" he whispered.

"Aye," she mumbled. "You're like a peat fire."

Elanta put a cup of hot water infused with valerian into Drosten's hand and tiptoed away. He brought it to Mhoire's lips. She took a swallow and raised her eyes to his face. It was haggard, the skin drawn tight against his bones, his eyes deep in their sockets.

"What's wrong?" she asked.

He smiled slightly. "Nothing now, *mo milidh*." He pressed the cup to her lips again, and she took another sip. But when he tried to get her to drink a third time, she shook her head and turned her face back into his shoulder.

He put down the cup and tentatively began to stroke her back. When she didn't rebel, he let his hand gently roam over her, soothing the muscles of her neck and her spine. She listened to his heart thumping in his chest, slow and regular.

He spoke into her ear: "Do you remember what happened, *mo milidh*?"

She nodded. "Fighting." Then she shuddered, recalling the dull thud of weapon against weapon and the screech of murder and chaos. "Was anyone killed?"

"A dozen Britons. Two of my men. Brendan and Corrac."

"I'm sorry."

His lips brushed her hair. "You saved my life, *mo milidh*. Everyone's."

She squeezed her eyes tight. In her mind's eye, she was on the wall again. Angry, hurling her rage and her arrows. Until the white-hot pain ripped through her body.

"Do you remember what else happened?" Drosten asked gently.

She took a deep breath and felt a tug of pain in her shoulder. "Aye."

"What do you remember?" He stroked her lower back.

"Pain. Heat."

"Aye. I pulled an arrow from your shoulder. The wound turned bad. You burned with fever." He paused. "The priest was here. Do you remember?"

A fog of drowsiness crept over her. The valerian was taking effect, and so was the lull of Drosten's heartbeat and his patient hand.

"The priest gave me the sacrament."

"Two sacraments." Drosten bent his head and tried to look into her eyes. She turned her face into his chest so that he couldn't.

"Aye." Her voice was muffled by the cloth. "He married us." She drew a shaky breath. The wound tugged and her chest burned. "I thought I was going to die. I'm so sorry, Drosten."

She felt him stiffen.

"I thought it was the right thing to do," she whispered. And then sleep stole her away.

At the edge of the woods, a man sat stiffly on his horse, hidden by a tangle of gorse bushes bursting with flowers. With a slow, keen eye, he surveyed Dun Darach on its shelf of land at the edge of the sea.

She had thwarted him again. A banshee woman who would not be killed. He gripped the reins, and his horse reared. Gritting his teeth, he hauled on the horse's mouth and forced the frightened animal to quiet down. Nay, he mustn't let his anger show, mustn't waste it. He must conserve the emotion, let it build, until he could unleash it properly.

Chapter Twenty

It took a month for Mhoire's wound to heal. A second month passed before they could get her to leave her bed.

The women gave her everything they had on hand to help her recover: milk in which a curing stone had been boiled, daily doses of meadowsweet, mugwort, and dandelion water, and as many warm blankets as she could stand. On her wound, they kept a plaster of plantain, and then bee resin, carefully collected by Grainne from a buzzing hive.

The wound healed well. Mhoire's spirit, however, was not so easily restored. She ate only when pressed, spoke only when spoken to. Day after day, she sat on a bench in the courtyard with her hands folded in her lap and an ocean of sadness in her eyes.

What was her life to be now?

She was defeated. That was the truth of it. Nay, that wasn't the truth. She had given everything up. And willingly, to save the women from harm. She had handed over Dun Darach to Drosten. She just hadn't thought she would live to see him take it.

And now he was in charge. She heard him and his men every day that she sat on the bench: building, repairing, planting a new crop, taking over. Taking over the women too. She could hear the men and women flirting. Every gay note stabbed her heart.

Mhoire filled her lungs with air. One might say that all

that had happened was very logical. Women married men. Men took charge. Together, they created order, although, she thought wryly, the hall was somewhat less than orderly now that the women's attentions were distracted from household duties. Aye, to most observers, life at Dun Darach had fallen very sensibly into place.

Except for two things.

Mhoire clasped her hands tightly in her lap and gazed blankly at a sky spotted with innocent white clouds.

She no longer felt she belonged here.

And she had a husband who hardly ever spoke to her.

Every time Drosten climbed the ladder to the roof of the small stone building, he could see Mhoire across the courtyard, motionless and alone. He had watched her closely these last two months. He had seen her withstand extreme physical pain with dogged endurance, her face drained of color and a sheen of sweat on her forehead. He had observed her first wobbly steps. And now, every time he reached the top of the ladder, he saw the sadness that bore down on her like a fist.

She looked fragile and vulnerable and lost, and he could hardly endure it. Every inch of his being wanted to take her to a private, protected place where he could soothe her and make her smile. Where he could kiss away the marks of strain around her eyes. Stroke her body until it thrummed with energy.

But he recognized her sadness for what it was. The deep agony of losing what was most precious.

Because of him.

Nay, the best good he could do, he figured, was to not make her grief worse with his presence.

He had thrown himself into repairing the fort. They had rebuilt the more important structures first. Now they were putting roofs on the smaller ones, including the small stone building that was to be Drosten and Mhoire's bedchamber.

Tension was ever-present. Everyone knew that at any moment they could be attacked again. There was sexual tension, too. The Pictish warriors were here to stay now, and scarcely a day went by when Drosten didn't notice one of his men paired off with one of the women.

He hoisted the bundle of reeds off his shoulder and laid it onto one of the beams that criss-crossed the roof. Lost in thought, he handled the feather-light reeds absent-mindedly. When a gust of wind whipped around the court-yard, half the bundle slipped through the timbers and fell to the ground.

"Damnation!" Drosten gazed down through the rungs as the reeds began to scatter.

"Nasty wind today," Alfred remarked from his perch on one of the crossbeams.

Drosten snatched up the wayward stalks and climbed up the ladder again. "The wind's a demon," he muttered.

"The demon's over there." Alfred gestured across the courtyard with his chin.

"I wouldn't call her a demon."

"She's haunting you."

Drosten did not reply.

Alfred reached for one of the ropes that was secured to the main beam to keep the thatching in place. "You should be happy. You've gotten what you wanted."

"And what is that?"

"This place. A wife."

"She's not been that."

Alfred yanked on the rope. "But she will be. Soon as this roof is finished."

Drosten stared at his hands. When the bedchamber was ready for occupancy, he and Mhoire would have to face each other. And he dreaded it.

"A little privacy will take care of things."

Drosten shook his head. "She married me out of duty, friend."

"You married *her* out of duty, didn't you?"

"Aye. But duty's poor purpose for a marriage."

Alfred snorted. "Now you're sounding just like her."

Aye, Drosten thought ruefully, Mhoire had been right

from the start. Obligation was the most common motive for marriage, and here they were, dutifully married. And miserable. He spread the reeds along the roof and began to tie them down.

"Well, we have worse things to worry about," Drosten said.

"The Britons, you mean."

"Aye, although I'm not certain it was the Britons who attacked us. Why would they come after Dun Darach now? These women have been alone for a year."

"So they assumed they could have it any time. When we arrived and spoiled their plan, they decided to drive us out."

"Maybe."

"And there was that attack on you when you were out hunting. That seemed typical of those bastards. Sneaking as they are."

Drosten shook his head. "Why would they single me out? Killing me might have caused confusion here, but it wouldn't have given them the fort. Not with the rest of you around to defend it." He looked at Alfred. "So, the question is, who *would* get Dun Darach more easily if I wasn't alive?"

"Irwin?"

"Perhaps. But if it was him, we're safe now. Mhoire will likely divorce me and marry him. There's no need left for him to kill me." Drosten fumbled with the ropes. Divorce was a common practice among both the Picts and the Scots, even though the church didn't approve of it.

"Mhoire's not going to divorce you, man."

"Of course she is."

"Nay. You're melting for her. No woman can resist that."

"Melting? I've hardly said five words to the woman in the last two months."

"And that's the proof of it. We could catapult a cow with the tension that's between the two of you."

"You're daft."

"She married you, didn't she?"

"She thought she was dying. She never believed she'd recover and be saddled with me."

"And do you remember nothing of that kiss she gave you? When she sewed up your arm?"

"Should I?"

"I'd want to."

"And why is that?"

"Well, I'm beginning to think I'd fancy a kiss like that myself from the right woman."

Drosten gaped at his friend, who, he noticed, was gazing at a tall, bony figure who had just stepped into the courtyard with a wash bucket in her hand.

"You're joking. Grainne?"

"What of her? She's loyal. Tough. Like your woman."

"Like boot leather."

"Aye," Alfred said with a note of awe. "Quite a woman she is."

Mhoire heard the skittering of pebbles and turned her head to see Elanta and Oran coming around the corner of the gathering hall. Each carried a bowl. Oran's, Mhoire surmised, held some sort of liquid, for the child shuffled along carefully, staring intently into it as if willing the contents not to slosh over the rim.

When she reached the spot where Mhoire was sitting, a grin of relief lit her face. "I've brought you something. Here." She held out the bowl.

"What is it?"

"Goose broth. Drink it. It will make you strong." Oran pushed the bowl a little closer to Mhoire's face.

Mhoire wrinkled her nose. "Why don't you drink it, Oran?"

"I'm strong already. But you're weak. That's what Grandmother says. She says your heart is hurting you, and it's not getting better because you're so weak."

"I see." Anger flickered in Mhoire's chest. They were talking about her.

"Please drink it."

Mhoire saw the disappointment in Oran's face and relented. The broth, warm and oily, slid like a worm into her belly.

Elanta sat down beside her. "Oran, my love," she said, "go help your grandmother."

Oran made a little pout but scampered off.

Mhoire ran her thumb along the rim of the bowl of goose broth that rested in her lap.

"So you all think I'm weak, do you?"

"Well, you're not moving around very much, are you?"

"And what is there for me to do? I see the Picts doing all the building, and you women doing all the chores, and Drosten directing everything, and soon all of you will be marrying these men and having babies, and quite honestly, I can't see what there is left for me to occupy my time with."

Elanta gave Mhoire a long, inscrutable look. Then she pressed her lips together and glanced away.

"You are marrying Brian, aren't you?" Mhoire asked.

"Aye, I am."

"How can you, Elanta? Have you no loyalty to Oran's father? You said you loved him, and yet only one year past his death, you are marrying another man."

"You think that marrying Brian means I did not love my husband? Neill was my beloved." She leaned toward Mhoire. "But he is dead. And I have a daughter to care for, and I will not let her suffer. That—*that*—would be a betrayal of her father."

Mhoire looked away.

"Do you know what it is like to be hungry, Mhoire? Desperately hungry? You feel faint all the time, and it seems as if there is a rat gnawing in your belly. But my little girl never complained. All last winter, when we picked frozen berries from the shrubs and searched through broken beechnut shells for the one or two nuts the animals hadn't gotten, she never cried or begged for food. She just got thinner and thinner. I won't let her starve like that again."

Mhoire stared at the sky, at the sea, at the stone wall that surrounded them. "Do you love Brian?" she finally asked.

"He's a good man, and I like him. But I don't love him the way you love Drosten." Elanta shook her head. "You have so much, Mhoire, and you don't even realize it. You love Drosten, and he loves you."

"Nay . . ."

"Aye. He loves you. He loves you to distraction. He loves you as deeply as a man can love a woman."

Color mottled Mhoire's pale skin. "His men say he is pretending."

"Pretending? Open your eyes! God in Heaven, he's barely left your side since the moment he saw you. He would break his own bones for you. He'd do anything, *anything*, to keep you safe and make you happy."

"You're mistaken."

"I know what a man in love looks like."

Mhoire gripped the bowl. "I forced him to marry me."

"Are you mad? He wants you."

"Then why doesn't he talk to me?"

"Because he's afraid. He sees how miserable you are, and he assumes it's because you can't bear being married to him."

Mhoire's flush deepened. "And so what kind of life is it to be reigned by a man?"

Elanta looked her in the eye. "Love can feel like a chain sometimes, Mhoire. But it offers freedom, too. When you're with a man, a man you love, a part of you that you never knew existed comes alive. And that—*that*—is really what you came to Dun Darach for. It wasn't independence you were seeking, Mhoire. It was life."

Just as Mhoire opened her mouth to reply, Oran skipped up to them.

"I've finished helping Grandmother," she announced. "What are you doing?"

"Talking." Elanta turned to her daughter.

"Oh. So what are you going to do now?"

"I'm not sure. Mhoire, what are you going to do now?"

Mhoire looked blank.

"You might collect reeds for baskets," Elanta said, "or you could help us wind heather into rope. Or perhaps you would like to find Drosten and tell him how to arrange your bedchamber. It's a woman's right to take charge of the household."

"I know," Oran interjected. "You must kiss him."

"What?"

The child nodded firmly. "Then he'll do whatever you want him to do."

"Oran, I don't think so."

"Aye," she answered, nodding again. "He will. That's what my mother did with Brian. She kissed him, and now he does whatever she says."

Chapter Twenty-one

Mhoire tried to plunge back into her familiar, depressed state, but her mind wouldn't cooperate. She couldn't keep her eyes off Drosten, who moved with animal-like grace on the roof across the courtyard.

She scurried into the gathering hall and laid down on her pallet. But still he filled up her mind. His deep, masculine voice. His golden hair. His guileless smiles. His soft, welcoming mouth that, for the brief moment it was fused with hers, had made every inch of her body come alive.

He loves you. He would do anything for you.

"Mother of God, I'm going daft!" she muttered to herself and scrambled to her feet. She had to move. Do something.

She launched herself out of the hall and across the courtyard. Before she knew it, she was at the open door of her new bedchamber. Wringing her hands, she stood uncertainly on the threshold. Then she tiptoed inside.

It was small, but a long, narrow window let in light. The cobwebs had been cleaned out, and the stone walls scrubbed. Furnishings were sparse: There was just the bed, which looked much too small to Mhoire's eyes, especially when she imagined Drosten's large body lying on it next to hers.

She bit her lip and turned away, and her eyes fell on Drosten's pack and his weapons stashed carelessly in a corner. There was something about the casual heap, its bulk, its hardness, and its aggressive import, that was so obviously masculine, it made her knees buckle.

She heard a scraping noise and looked up sharply. Drosten was bending his head to get through the doorway. In his hands was a leather bag. Her bag.

Her heart pattered against her ribs like hail on a roof.

"Elanta asked me to bring this." He waved the bag in her direction.

"I see."

"Where would you like me to put it?"

"Oh. Well . . ." She looked around the chamber and when her eyes again landed on Drosten's pack, they darted away. She couldn't put *her* bag next to *his*. "Perhaps just on the bed for now."

He took the few steps to the bed and lowered the bag onto the coverlet. "Thank you," she said, as he straightened.

They lapsed into silence.

Think of something to say, she commanded herself. But all she could think of was Oran's directive: *Kiss him*.

He was saying something.

"What?" Lord, she was losing her mind *and* her hearing.

"I said, are you pleased with this chamber?"

Mhoire's eyes skimmed the room. The ceiling caught her attention, and she frowned.

Drosten followed her gaze and shifted uncomfortably on his big feet. "Aye, well—" He cleared his throat. "The roof still needs a little patching. I see that it's a bit thin in that area, but, uh, I'll cut more reeds for it tomorrow."

Mhoire looked at him.

"Tonight," he added quickly. "There's plenty of light yet. I'll patch it up tonight."

She eyed him thoughtfully. He looked terribly uncomfortable. Contrite even. Not sure of what to make of him, she returned to examining the room. This time her gaze lingered on the window shutters.

Drosten's brows lowered. He walked past her to the window, so close she felt the air stir. He peered at the shutters, and then fingered the latch, which was hanging loosely by a single nail.

"I, uh—" He turned. "I don't know what's happened here. The other nail must have come loose, you see. Just one more nail—" He gestured with his hand. "—one more nail and it'll be stout as can be. I can do that tomorrow. Er, tonight! I can do that tonight as well."

He was close. So close she could smell him. A delicious smell of muscle and skin and the outdoors. A warm smell that was all Drosten.

Kiss him.

Her eyes traveled to his neck. The laces of his tunic were undone, and he had no shirt on. She could see the golden hairs of his chest and underneath them, dark-brown splotches of mud.

"You've already worked hard today," she murmured.

"It doesn't matter. This would be no trouble."

Kiss him.

She brought her hand to his chest and pulled the cloth of the tunic aside. "You're all scars," she said, frowning.

She felt him take a deep, shuddering breath before answering.

"Those are just old battle scars." He paused. "Do they disgust you?"

"Nay." He was beautiful, every inch of him. Fine skin over hard muscle over strong bone.

Her gaze traveled to his arms. The sleeves of his tunic had been torn off, and his arms were bare to the shoulder. She touched the spot where he had recently been stabbed. The wound had healed, but it had left a scar—a white ridge of flesh with little white points on both sides that marked where her needle had taken its stitches.

"Does this hurt when you use your arm?"

"Nay."

Kiss him.

Mhoire looked up at Drosten's face. His eyes were closed and his expression strained. She dropped her hand. Maybe he didn't want her to touch his scars.

Maybe she should concentrate on learning how to manage a man first, and save kissing him for later.

"Um, I was wondering, Drosten . . ."

"Hmm?" He opened his eyes. They were so close she could see little specks of brown in the blue irises.

"I was wondering if you might help me bring in the rest of my things. It's hard for me to lift anything heavy."

He blinked a few times and then looked—this was curious—pleased. "I would be happy to."

His eyes traveled over her face and her neck and down to the bodice of her dress, which was cut low enough that, from his height, he could easily see the swells of her breasts. "I'll patch the roof and fix the shutters and carry in all your things." His voice was low and mesmerizing.

She gulped.

The ground seemed to roll beneath Mhoire's feet as she walked across the courtyard from the bedchamber back to the gathering hall. Once inside, she groped through the dimness to her pallet and sat down with a thump. She wiped her sweating brow with her sleeve and smoothed her hair behind her ears. Then she blinked a few times and stared into space.

She didn't notice Brigit's curious stare or Elanta's smug half-smile.

"I'd be happy to carry anything you want me to."

"I'll do it tonight."

"He'd break his bones for you."

Kiss him!

She shivered.

Why was she shivering when she was so hot?

She rubbed her sleeve over her cheeks and the back of her neck. Mother of God, the hall was stifling!

She stood, grabbed a willow basket from the floor, and wobbled toward the door.

She would gather herbs, that's what she would do. Most of the healing plants she had brought with her from Ireland had already been used—on her—and it would be wise to restock the supply. Now that it was spring, many helpful plants would be in flower.

She headed for the gate in the outer wall. It was so much cooler outside. Out here she could breathe. She would collect plants now, and later she would think about Drosten, and why it was that his mere presence made her faint.

She waded through the slender grasses at the base of the fort. Above her, meadowlarks swooped and sang.

Ah, thyme! She smelled it on the air before she saw it. Bending, she plucked a sprig and held it to her nose. Thyme was the plant of kings and princes, with an aromatic scent that bestowed courage and strength. She felt a need for courage. She tucked the sprig into her bodice. Then she gathered a few more stalks and dropped them into her basket.

She scanned the meadow. A clump of meadowsweet was just ahead. Meadowsweet was a cure for fevers and headaches. She picked two handfuls.

Butterwort. A magical plant. She could give some to the cow so that fairies wouldn't spoil the milk. Butterwort protected people from fairies, too. Mhoire plucked a dozen of the small yellow flowers and slipped a sprig into her bodice alongside the thyme.

She straightened and looked around. A light breeze, smelling faintly of the sea, lifted the tendrils of hair near her face. Common sense told her she should return to the fort. She glanced over her shoulder, hoping to see one of Drosten's men following her. But no one was in sight.

She turned and faced the woods. So alluring they were, green and thick. Shaking off her fear, she stepped into them.

It was cool under the trees. The oak and hawthorn leaves filtered the heat of the sun. The evening light beamed down in long, slender rays. Sprays of ferns unfurled here and there, yellow-green in their newness.

Just at her feet, she caught a glimpse of wood sorrel. She bent and plucked a stalk and nibbled on it. Wood sorrel would be handy to have. It made a good poultice for wounds, and Lord knew they would need that. And it improved the appetite. Maybe it would help her get more food into her stomach.

She was deep in the woods now. Here, beyond the reach of the wind, nothing moved. The oaks stood steady. Even the birds had grown silent.

Suddenly, a twig snapped. Her head sprung up.

Drosten.

"I saw you leave the fort alone," he said. "I was worried."

He stood in shadow. Tall and solid as the trees around him. She could just make out his face. Tension furrowed his brow. His voice sounded rough. From what? From worry? Worry about her?

She took a few steps toward him and bent her head upwards to look into his eyes.

"I didn't know where you were going . . ." he continued in a voice like sand. "I thought someone had better keep an eye on you."

She stood just inches from him. Close enough to feel his heat. She laid her hand on his bare arm. It was warm and furry with his golden hair.

He spoke again. "*Mo milidh*, this is so hard for me."

She looked into his eyes. So dark they were. Dark and tortured.

"I think of you constantly," he whispered.

She raised her hand and laid it against his cheek. His eyes widened slightly, like those of a wild stallion unused to human touch.

She rubbed her thumb against his lower lip. It was full and warm but parched from the sun. Rough, yet soft. Like him.

She smiled into his eyes. She saw wonder in them and a question. Slowly, watching, looking for her answer, he bent his mouth to hers.

The first touch was light, too light. Too brief. When he pulled away, she gripped the collar of his tunic and tugged him back to her.

Her lips pressed against his. She reached up to his tousled hair, to his neck, damp with sweat. Her arms circled his broad shoulders. Then she slid her mouth away and buried her face in his neck. What was this—this need? This longing. This storm of desire that filled her and drove her forward. To where? To what?

He kissed her ear. She lifted her gaze to his.

His eyes were smiling. He ran them over her face, looking. Looking at her. He ran his finger along her eyebrow, down her cheek. Exploring, taking her in, learning her with his touch. He met her eyes again, smiled a deeper smile.

He was calm now, a pool of warmth, a pool that surrounded her, bathed her in warmth. Above her, birds chirped their evening song. The wind soughed quietly in the trees. The forest breathed.

She stood as still as a heron. What should she do? Lord, she didn't know anything about this kind of behavior! What should she do?

Her pulse quickened, a note of panic. But his hold was steady, strong.

He kissed her until the marrow of her bones melted.

Sometime later, they stumbled back to the fort, under a turquoise sky fading into evening's pale gray, and drifted into the gathering hall. They ate quietly, responding to the curious looks of the others with telling flushes.

"You want me," he accused her with a smile, leaning close.

"Aye," she breathed, smiling back.

"You're not afraid of me?"

"Nay, not you."

"What then?"

Uncertain, she didn't answer.

Chapter Twenty-two

A tap on the door woke Drosten just before dawn. It took a moment for him to realize where he was. He wasn't used to beds, nor to having a warm, feminine body close to his.

The knock came again, and with a grimace of annoyance, he rolled noiselessly onto his feet.

He opened the door. Alfred stood on the other side, and the look on his face told Drosten there was serious business to be dealt with.

He reached for his tunic and tugged it over his head.

"Britons?" he asked, as he slipped outside. Alfred shook his head.

Drosten's hand tightened on his axe. "Danes?"

"There's a courier."

They crossed the courtyard to the fort's outer gate under a sky still heavy with stars. A pine-knot torch had been jammed into an iron ring in the wall. Standing within its flaring, yellow glow was a young man splattered with mud.

"Speak," Drosten said.

"I have a message from your father."

"Say it."

The young man licked his lips. "In the words of Gormach mac Nectan, you are to kill Mhoire ni Colman."

Drosten's head snapped back. "You are mistaken. Mhoire ni Colman is my wife. I sent a message to my father weeks ago telling him of the marriage."

159

"Gormach mac Nectan says that now you are married and have possession of Dun Darach, you must get rid of the woman. Those are his orders."

Drosten grabbed the courier by his shirt and breathed into his face. "If you think I will harm her, you had better change your mind before I bash your head against the wall."

The courier paled.

Drosten breathed hard and released his hold. He knew his father hated the Scots and the Irish both. *And so it has come to this.* Because Gormach mac Nechtan cares more about the survival of his people than the life of one person. Or the happiness of his son.

The roar rose in his throat. It came from the boy who had lost all things innocent and kind. It grew as losses grow, consuming his spirit. And it tore from the man as the callous of time was ripped from him, and all he could see was his mother's bloodless face and his sister's mouth screaming with terror.

"Nay!" he cried, and brought his fists to his eyes.

He willed himself to think. Never would he harm Mhoire. Never.

He knew what he must do.

He must renounce her. That was the only chance he had to protect her. He must leave Dun Darach, sever the marriage. For if there was no marriage, there would be no alliance between the Picts and the Scots, and the only way the Picts could take Dun Darach would be by force. Drosten had to hope that his father would not start a war with the Scots while the Danes were burning his fields.

He would pay a price for his disobedience, Drosten knew that. By sabotaging his father's plans, he would lose all his status in the clan, perhaps even be exiled. A leader should be cold-blooded, his family would say. But he could not allow another woman whom he loved to die.

Mhoire stretched as a cat stretches, languidly, from the center outwards. Her body felt different this morning. It was as if every nerve had been touched by a hazel wand and magically brought to life.

Sleepily, she turned on her side and opened her eyes. Drosten was gone. Mhoire inched herself across the bed and buried her nose in the hollow of the pillow where he had rested his head.

He had brought to their bed the same mixture of gentleness and directness that characterized all his other dealings with her. She had never had anyone give her such complete attention. His willingness—nay, his desire—to be fully occupied with her and her alone, seized her affections.

But where would love lead?

A whistle of birdsong, close, made her jump. A robin, its breast plumped, sat on the window ledge. It bobbed its head here and there, and perused her with a bright black eye.

Her life had taken a turn she never had anticipated. She had fallen in love with the man she had hoped to be free of. And now she wanted so much to be with him. How could that have happened?

She had been lonely. Now she had companionship.

She had been fearful. Now she had hope.

She had craved freedom. Now she had love.

She had felt hollow. And now—now she was full. And happy.

Perhaps what she had thought was emptiness was simply life waiting to be born.

The robin's wings fluttered. As quick as a blink, it flew off the ledge and away. Mhoire sat up and gave her head a shake. *What would life be like now?* Well, the only practical way to answer that, she told herself, was to climb out of bed and find out.

She was disappointed but not surprised that Drosten was nowhere in sight. She had never had a husband before and did not know what to expect of one. Her own father had disappeared for days on end without a word to her mother. Mhoire didn't think Drosten would be that unfeeling, but she also knew that he wasn't the type of man who would ask for her permission before heading off.

She busied herself with household chores. For an hour, she wove baskets of sedge and honeysuckle. Then, feeling restless, she went down to the beach and collected seaweed and blueberries.

Her shoulder wound, she was happy to discover, did nothing more than pinch as long as she did not extend her arm too far. But there was another feeling that was not so controllable. *Didn't he want to see her after such a momentous night together?*

She would sew. Sewing calmed her nerves. Intent on retrieving her needle and thread, she marched into her bedchamber. And it was then that she felt the first glimmer of anxiety. Drosten's pack was missing from its spot in the corner, along with every weapon that he owned.

She emerged from the chamber as if from a fog, seeing things she should have noticed earlier. Alfred, for example, who often accompanied Drosten on an expedition, was crouched by himself in the courtyard, shaping arrowheads out of quartz.

She approached him as calmly as she could. "Alfred, do you know where Drosten has gone off to?"

He didn't look up. "Nay. Can't say that I do."

"Did he go hunting?"

"Didn't notice."

"But you saw him this morning?"

Alfred hesitated. "Aye."

"He didn't tell you where he was going?"

The man didn't answer, but his hands stopped moving.

"Alfred . . ." She struggled to keep her voice steady. "You know something that you are not telling me. What is it?"

Alfred pinched his lips together, and his brows lowered.

"Alfred . . ." Panic was rising now.

"He made me swear not to tell you."

"Made you swear?"

"He's left. That's all."

"*Left?* What do you mean?"

Slowly, Alfred stood. "I mean he's gone from the fort. Gone from Dun Darach." He threw down the grinding stone he held in his hand and wiped his brow with his sleeve. "He won't be back."

Mhoire swayed on her feet. "I don't understand," she said, her voice high and thin. "Why would he leave?"

Alfred's shoulders sagged, but he kept his voice strong. "He's going to divorce you. He instructed me to tell you that later, this evening, when he was full away."

"Divorce me?"

"Aye." Alfred glanced away and back again.

"And he's gone alone?"

"Aye."

Behind her, there was the sound of shuffling feet. Some of the others, the soldiers and the women, had come into the courtyard.

Mhoire shook her head. This didn't make sense. "He's divorcing me, but he has left all of his soldiers here. Why?" She looked up at the big man, and this time her intelligence dared him to lie. "Why alone?"

"I cannot tell you."

"You must tell me!" She stamped her foot, furious. "I command you to tell me! He is my husband and I am mistress of this fort. He has left you here and all these men, and you are clearly under my control." She was shouting now. "You must tell me!"

Grief poured into his eyes. "He has gone back to his clan."

"His clan? Why in the name of Mary would he do that and leave you here?"

Alfred stood silent.

He was tall, almost as tall as Drosten, but Mhoire remembered Drosten's instructions. *Come from below.* In an instant, she had her dagger out and at Alfred's throat.

"It's a small weapon, but it will cut nonetheless." She pressed the tip against Alfred's skin. Then she made herself ask the question that was tearing at her. "Is it another woman?"

Alfred looked down at the dagger. "Nay. A courier arrived before dawn. From his father."

"And what was the message?"

"Drosten was told to kill you."

The others gasped. Mhoire stared into Alfred's eyes and saw the pain of truth there. She lowered the dagger. "Because they don't need me now. Because I am a Scot," she said flatly. "Because Drosten is a Pictish prince, and Gormach mac Nechtan does not want to sully the Pictish blood by bringing a Scot into his family."

"Aye. All of that is true. But Drosten won't hurt a woman. Especially you. Even for his father." Alfred's features blurred around the edges, as if his warrior's strength was draining from him.

Draining into Mhoire.

Her jaw set. "They'll shame him if he breaks the marriage and loses the land. Or banish him." She looked Alfred square in the face. "And I'm not going to let that happen. I'm going to stop this foolishness before it goes any farther."

Alfred shook his head. "You can't. This is the only way Drosten can save you. His father would not dare attack you and seize Dun Darach for fear of retaliation from the king of Dal Riata. Drosten said he wants you to have what you always wanted. This place. He wants you to live your dreams."

"So he'll throw away his future? That's his scheme?"

"It's the only scheme possible. You can't stop it."

Mhoire squared her shoulders and lifted her chin. "The truth can stop it. So the truth will be told." She turned and found Grainne in the crowd. "Bring me my arrows and my bow."

Chapter Twenty-three

The sky had sheathed itself with clouds by the time Drosten reached the hills at the northern end of the island. His first task was to find the priest that had married them and demand a divorce. Normally, a Pict seeking divorce would secure one from the Pictish court of law, but in this case, his influential father would make that impossible. Nay, the priest was his only hope, though God in heaven knew what grounds Drosten could come up with to convince the church to sever the marriage. One could argue that a dowry was smaller than promised, or the bride was not a virgin. But it wasn't in Drosten's nature to lie. And his mind, ordinarily clever and quick, was so dulled by grief that it couldn't devise anything subtle. He guessed he would have to resort to intimidation.

He headed into a glen. The mist settled in his hair and lay cold against his face. Icy rivulets of water slipped under the collar of his cloak and down his neck. Shivering from the wetness, he sat half-bent in the saddle. Fleetingly, he thought of finding shelter and building a fire. But he took no action. For he knew that the chill that racked his body came from his soul.

For nigh on twenty years, he had borne the guilt of his mother's death. All these years, he had sought to make up for his sin: through loyalty to his clan and protectiveness toward his people, even through his dogged resolve to shelter Mhoire from harm.

But the guilt never went away. It was a mark upon him, like the paintings pricked into his skin that could not be erased even if scoured with the roughest stone.

But now, now he could rid himself of it. This was his chance for redemption.

He wouldn't see Mhoire again. He would give up the marriage. He would give up, too, all his hopes for leadership. And it could be worse. His father could easily decide to banish him to some monastery clinging to a rock in the sea. Perhaps he should banish himself. First, divorce. Then, exile. He would sacrifice his life for that of the woman he loved, something he should have done all those years before.

Drosten heaved a breath that was close to a sob. Where was the joy in redemption? Why was it filled with so much pain?

His horse stumbled, and the sudden movement jerked him to awareness. He mustn't fall off his horse and break his neck, at least not yet. If he died before divorcing Mhoire, his father would take over Dun Darach and simply arrange to have her married to another Pict. That thought, if none else, forced Drosten to carry on.

He patted his horse's neck with his large hand and coaxed it forward. When they came to a small waterfall, he directed it to a firm spot next to the water where it could bend its shaggy head and drink.

Lady's mantle nodded in the rush of air. The tiny green blossoms reminded him of the herbs that Mhoire had tucked beside her breast the evening he had made love to her. His heart tightened.

Then the world exploded.

The blow came from behind and would have killed him, except that his horse, more alert than he was, flinched and, ears back, skittered sideways.

The axe grazed his thigh. He reacted as thousands of encounters had taught him. With a series of smooth, violent movements, he had his own axe in his hand, one foe dead on the ground, and the other more than an arm's length away from him. But the second man was quick and ready. He spurred his horse directly at Drosten, and their weapons crossed with a clang. The assailant was heavy and experienced, and in other circumstances it would have been a close match. But Drosten had passion to draw upon and a transcendent desperation to have the last days of his life play out right.

With inhuman force, he drove his axe forward until his assailant yielded his hold. And then he took him down with a single blow. The violence of Drosten's thrust made his horse stumble, and with an uncontrolled slide and a hideous thud, Drosten was on the ground. A burst of pain turned the world white, and then he was consumed by darkness.

Mhoire was unstoppable. She knew what she wanted, and like an arrow shot with such force that neither wind nor man could distract it, she hurled herself toward her goal: to find Drosten.

The women murmured misgivings. *She would be captured, raped, killed. Or she'd fall prey to fever. The rain is coming down in buckets.*

Alfred argued. *Drosten had made his decision, and it would be impossible to change his mind. The forces at work are larger than her, larger than him. Larger than love.*

She saddled her horse herself, mounted, and wrapped her cloak about her. Then she addressed the assembled warriors, stone-faced.

"I need three men."

A gust of wind blew from the mountains and skittered pebbles across the courtyard.

Brian nodded and trotted, grim-faced, toward the stable. Fergus lumbered after him.

Mhoire stared down at Alfred, who stood with his chin lowered. Finally, he shot her a dark gaze. She tugged on her reins and whirled her horse toward the gate, trailing dust behind her.

Alfred watched her leave. Then he headed toward the stable and found his mount.

They spied Drosten's horse first, standing in the wind-flattened grass of the glen. Instincts bred of long companionship had kept the beast near its master. As Mhoire and the men approached, it blew softly through its nose, glad for company.

Mhoire slipped off her horse and fell to her knees at Drosten's side.

His lips were blue, and his face the color of parchment. She bent her head and lay her ear against his cold mouth. A slight breath tickled her skin. She placed her hand under his ear. A pulse. Rapid but regular.

"He's alive," she said.

Quickly, she explored his body, feeling for fractures and looking for wounds. The hair on the back of his head was matted with blood, but otherwise he was sound.

"He's cracked his head, and the cold's taking him. We need to make a fire."

"Aye, but not here," Alfred replied. He looked at Fergus and Brian, who had just finished examining the two dead bodies lying in the grass. "We'd best get away, before someone comes looking for them."

Alfred lifted Drosten's shoulders and Brian took his feet, and they draped him like a carpet over his horse.

Chapter Twenty-four

They found a cave farther up the glen—a long, vertical fissure in the rock wall, formed not by the sea but by some titantic heave of stone in the time of the ancients.

Brian took flint from his belt pouch and started a fire. They laid Drosten near it. Mhoire ran her hands over him more slowly and deliberately. She told herself she was checking for wounds, but in truth, she just needed to feel him, to touch his solid bulk.

She slipped a folded blanket under his head and smoothed back the hair from his brow. It was dark from the rain, like wet sand. Dark bruises lay under his eyes, and his skin looked transparent. Mhoire rubbed her hand along her cloak to warm her fingers and then laid them against his cold cheek.

He opened his eyes.

A tiny crease appeared between his brows. "Am I dead?" he whispered.

"Nay, my heart. I've found you."

The pucker deepened and suddenly his shoulders were off the ground. Mhoire pushed helplessly against him to keep him down. "Go back to the fort!" he yelled. "You must go back to the fort!"

Then Drosten recognized Alfred, and his thrashings and shouting intensified. "I told you to keep her there!" he thundered. "Take her back or I swear you'll have my sword in your gut!"

It took all three men to hold him down. He landed a kick on Brian's thigh. Grimacing, the young man held on. One arm came loose from Fergus's hold and an elbow connected with the older warrior's thick chest. For a moment, it seemed that Drosten in his rage would fling them off. But Mhoire hurled herself at him and captured his face with both hands. "Please, Drosten! Please listen! Please listen to me!" She dug in with her fingernails and held on stubbornly until he attended.

He turned agonized eyes to hers. "You must go home. Go back to Dun Darach. You'll be safe there."

She shook her head. "Nay, my heart. Dun Darach is not my home."

"It is. You don't understand. My father will kill you. I can stop him but only if you go back." He looked at her with a drowned blue gaze. "Marry Irwin. Try to be happy. Keep Dun Darach."

Tears filled her eyes. "My heart, I must tell you something." She ran her thumb over his lips to silence him, to calm him before the storm she herself had to bring. She let her gaze wander over the planes of his face, the line of his brows. Finally, she met his eyes and held them, and forced the words from her mouth: "Dun Darach does not belong to me. Colman is not my father." And then she dropped her hands.

Brian, Fergus, and Alfred released their hold and sat back, mouths open.

Mhoire bowed her head and folded her arms across her chest. She waited for Drosten's reaction.

"Leave us," he said to his men. They scrambled out of the cave.

The air stirred with their passing. For long seconds, the glow of the fire licked wildly along the stone walls and the bare ground, and then settled once more into a steady blaze.

When Mhoire looked up, Drosten was lying on his back again, watching her with exhausted, thoughtful eyes.

"Tell me, *mo milidh*," he said.

Her story was short. All she knew was that her mother

had become pregnant by another man, a man who was not Colman mac Morgand. Mhoire did not know who her true father was.

"How are you aware of this?" Drosten asked.

"My mother told me."

"And Colman? What does he know?"

"I'm not certain. Mother said it was our secret. Hers and mine. My fa . . . Colman never spoke of it." Mhoire wiped her palms on her skirt. Despite the cold of the cave, she was clammy with sweat. "I have acted deceitfully. I allowed Colman to arrange our marriage and bestow me with his land, even though I knew I was not his daughter. I have committed a great sin."

Drosten was silent.

"But I won't let you die for it." The words caught in her throat. "I was desperate to get away, and I thought I could live the lie. I did not think it would matter. In my heart, I had thought it was another reason not to marry you—since I wasn't Colman's daughter, I *shouldn't* marry you. And even though I couldn't reveal the truth, I still thought I was doing what was right. And then when I did marry you, I thought that was right, too, because it would mean the women would be safe." She lifted her eyes. "I didn't intend to live. I didn't mean to deceive you."

"That's why you said you were sorry you had married me."

Mhoire nodded. "I hated the fact that I had forced you into marrying a liar. Once again, I had tried to do something right and good, and it had turned out to be bad. I hate myself for that." She twisted her hands in her lap and looked up, her dark eyes shining and intense. "But I'm not completely sorry. I love you. With my body and my heart."

She took a deep breath and continued. "But I have put everyone in jeopardy. The women. Your soldiers. You. I won't let you die for my sake. I will tell your father that Dun Darach is not mine, and all this will end. The fighting. The marriage. Everything."

For a moment, Drosten watched her in silence. Somewhere deep in the cave, water dripped. Outside, darkness fell like a mantle.

"My father will imprison you," he finally said.

"Mayhap." Mhoire's teeth began to chatter. "Mayhap he will let me go."

"Go where?"

She had no answer. With her secret revealed, she could not return to Dun Darach, and she must not return to Ireland. Colman would kill her. She was a lone woman with no patronage, no land, no husband, and no hope.

Drosten lifted his hand. "Come here, *mo milidh*. Come lay by me."

A sob tore from her throat. "I can't."

"Please."

She shook her head. She fought the sobs until her throat ached. "It will be so hard to leave you, if I go near you now."

He stretched out his arm. "I'm shaking with cold. *Mo milidh*, I need you."

She saw the tremor in his hand and the blueness on his lips, and could not resist his plea. Crawling on her knees, she went to him. He tucked her against his shoulder, and folded his arms tightly about her. She gripped his tunic with her fist, and when he turned his face into her hair, she could not stop her tears.

They lay together for some time. The soldiers must have fed the fire, for whenever Mhoire opened her eyes, it was burning low and bright. She drifted in and out of sleep, but Drosten never seemed to. Each time her eyes fluttered open, he would stoke her back or kiss her hair. Once, he grazed her lips lightly with his. His tender gestures made her want to weep even more, but she denied the release. She could see the broken look in Drosten's eyes and dared not add her misery to his own. She realized then how highly strung he was—like a stallion, strong and muscled, and sensitive to the bone.

It was still deep dark when she roused herself and

brewed some yarrow tea. Quietly, they both drank from the same cup. When Drosten laid down, he coaxed her to his side again, and she drew her cloak, which had dried by the fire, over the both of them.

She laid her forehead against his.

He kissed her. His lips were warm and tender.

"Don't you hate me?" she whispered.

"How could I hate you, *mo milidh*?"

"Because I have done such a terrible thing."

"You tried to save yourself. There is no shame in that."

"But I have made everyone's life worse."

"You made mine infinitely better. I only wish I had had more than one night with you."

"Drosten . . ."

He kissed her again, more firmly. Then he laid his large hand against her cheek. "I won't let you sacrifice yourself for me, *mo milidh*."

"And I won't let you sacrifice yourself for me."

The words hung between them.

She raised her hand and buried her fingers in the soft hair next to his temple. Like eiderdown it was, strong and shining.

"Were those your father's men that sought to kill you?" she asked quietly.

"I didn't recognize any of them."

"Might he have hired them?"

"Mayhap. But I doubt my father was behind this attack. He would have known it would take more than two men to kill me. And he couldn't have realized so quickly that I had disobeyed his command. His courier is still at Dun Darach."

"Could one of your men be a spy? Could one of them have heard you say you wouldn't kill me and told your father?"

He shook his head. "Even if there was a spy among my men, he couldn't have gotten back to Pictland so soon to report my disobedience."

"Unless your father is near."

Drosten's face clouded.

"Who then, my heart, if not your father? Who would try to kill you?"

"I have many enemies, *mo milidh*." He smiled ruefully. "Though I must say, this one—whoever he is—is persistent."

"What do you mean?"

"He's tried to kill me three times now."

Mhoire's hand stilled. She withdrew it from Drosten's hair and rested it against his chest. "*Three* times?"

He looked amused by her state of shock. "Aye. First the stab in the arm . . ."

"When you went out alone . . ."

"Aye. You got me drunk and patched me up, *mo milidh*." He drew his face closer to hers and lightly kissed her temple and then her cheek. His lips skimmed the corner of her mouth. "Do you remember?"

"Aye," she breathed.

He kissed her again, on the mouth. Harder. Hotter.

"Do you know how much I wanted you then, *mo milidh*?"

"But . . ." She drew away, searched his eyes. "But you were drunk. I thought . . . you said you didn't remember anything." She looked down, confused and embarrassed all over again. "You didn't remember that I kissed you."

He tilted her head up, made her take in his words. "My memory may be faulty, but my desire was true. I wanted you from the minute I saw you, crawling out of that roof, with straw in your hair and a dagger in your mouth."

Mhoire pulled herself closer, wrapped her arms around his waist, and sunk her face into his shoulder.

She felt his breath on her hair and then his lips on her neck. They were drowning. They both were drowning. And these kisses were taking them down. Down to where the pain of loss would be forever unbearable.

But Mhoire couldn't bring herself to stop him.

She shuddered with wanting. Then she pulled in a breath and forced her mind back to their conversation.

"If this was the third time you were attacked, when was the second?"

"The raid on Dun Darach."

She drew back again, and looked into his eyes. "You think those men were after you?"

"Aye."

"But why?"

"If all they had wanted was the fort, they would simply have lit fire to the place and picked us off like mice running from a flaming haystack. But instead they came through the wall and sought me out."

"I thought that raid was just my bad luck."

"Perhaps I am your bad luck."

"It must be the Britons then. Irwin said they were near. And they've been fighting with you for years."

"Hmm."

"Who else could it possibly be? The Danes? Dear God, could it be the Danes?"

"Nay. The Danes have more barbaric ways of getting what they want." She heard the grief in his voice, the grief that was locked tight within him.

"You know them too well, don't you, my heart?" she asked gently.

"Aye." His body stiffened protectively.

"You know the worst they can do." Once again, her hand went to his hair, pushed it gently back from his brow. "Tell me about your mother."

His eyes closed. "Nay, *mo milidh*. I can't. I can't tell you that."

"You must."

His voice declined to a whisper. "You'll shun me. I couldn't bear it. Not now."

She waited two breaths. Three. He was silent.

"My heart, it will be better to say it aloud. Trust me. Trust how much I love you."

Two more breaths. Five. Seven.

Was he being stubborn? Drosten wasn't like that. Afraid?

Mhoire felt a spark of anger. "I've told you my secret. Tell me yours."

He studied her, saw how her mouth had hardened, and sat up. He picked up a piece of kindling and poked at the fire. "It was long ago."

Mhoire raised herself and tucked her feet under her skirt. "How old were you when it happened?"

"Seven years."

She waited.

"My father was away from home. He thought the fort was safe. He never believed the Danes would sail that far inland." Drosten's shoulders hunched, and he pushed at the fire as if to brighten the blaze. But Mhoire could see he wasn't truly paying attention to it. His mind was traveling back. Back to the horror.

"What happened?" she prompted softly.

"They had sailed up the river. It was nighttime. I was sleeping."

"But you heard them."

"I heard noises. Shouting. Screams." He shuddered. "I jumped out of bed and grabbed my dagger and ran to the window. There were fires everywhere. The roofs of all the buildings were burning. I didn't . . . understand. People were running, everywhere, back and forth, yelling. And the cows were bellowing. I kept thinking, what are they doing to the cows?" He shook his head, still amazed at his own foolish question, a child's question.

"And then the door burst open. I knew immediately that they were Danes. Huge men, huge shoulders and thick necks like bulls. They wore bright metal breastplates. For a minute I thought, 'Could they be angels?' But they were ugly. Horrible. With wild eyes and red mouths. I heard one of them say something, but the sounds weren't even like words." Drosten let the stick of wood in his hand fall, wrapped his arms low across his body, bent over them. "I flung the knife." His head swung back and forth, as if he couldn't believe what his mind's eye saw. "I missed."

Mhoire watched the muscle in the side of his face flex.

Then she inched closer, laid her hand on his arm. "My heart, you were only seven years old."

Drosten ran his hands over his face. His breath came in shivers.

"Where was your mother?" she asked, not sure any more if she wanted to know.

He shook his head.

She moved her hands to his. Took them in her own. Waited.

"She was in the hearth room. On her knees." Sweat beaded on his forehead. "Two men were holding her, one on each side. They had their hands on her shoulders. They had my sister Bria, as well. She was frightened. Almost out of her mind. She . . . We used to play together. And when she saw me, she began to cry and reached for me, but one of the men hit her hard across the face." Drosten paused, slipped his hands from hers, wiped his forehead with his sleeve. "She screamed, and then my mother screamed, and all I could think of was, I must stop them from hitting my sister. So I kicked one of the men who was holding me in the groin and for one blessed second I thought I could get away. But the other one rammed his fist into my nose. Then everything went black, and I could taste the blood streaming down my throat. I heard them laugh. And Bria screaming, and my mother . . . *Sweet God!*"

He squeezed his eyes shut, nearly doubled. Mhoire slipped her arm around his shoulders, leaned him against her, murmured words that were not words, only croonings more ancient than language.

Slowly Drosten gathered himself, drew back slightly but stayed within the circle of her arms. "They tied me to a chair."

He paused again.

"My mind came back, and I saw them take the torcs that were around their necks and put them on top of my mother's head and my sister's head. They thought that was funny. One of them—their leader, I think—spoke a bit of Pictish, and he kept saying, 'The Pictish queens have Danish crowns.' And then he turned to me and said, 'You are worth nothing.' "

Drosten took a shaky breath. "He knew, you see, that our royalty and our titles are handed down from mother to daughter. And then he said . . . then he said, 'You are too worthless to kill, Pictish boy.' "

Drosten closed his eyes for a moment. Opened them. Sweat dripped down his temples, wetting his hair. "He said, 'So we'll let you choose. We'll kill one of your queens and let the other one live. You choose.' "

He began to shake. Mhoire reached for his hands again, and he gripped them so hard she thought her fingers would break.

"I couldn't do it. I couldn't choose. I wouldn't say either name. They kept asking, over and over, who should live— my mother or my sister. I kept shaking my head. My whole body was shaking. My teeth were knocking against each other, and there was all this blood in my throat. I thought I was drowning in it. They hit me again and again. I don't know how many times."

He swallowed hard. "Finally I blacked out. The next morning someone found me still tied to the chair. They said the Danes were gone, and they had taken my sister with them. And . . . and my mother . . . my mother . . ." His face twisted. ". . . had hung herself in the night."

Mhoire pulled him close, anchored him. Her tears fell like rain in his hair.

Finally, she spoke. "She spared you, my heart. She made the choice you could not make."

"I never would have spoken. I never would have given in."

"She knew that."

"They could have tortured me. I never would have yielded."

"She knew that, my heart. Your mother knew you. She knew how strong you were, even at seven. She could not bear the thought of your being harmed. She killed herself to prevent it."

"I didn't want her to die . . ."

"Nay, my heart. Of course you did not."

"I should have done something. I should have taken better aim with the knife. Or had my axe ready. Or tricked them somehow. Had some strategy. Something . . ."

"There was nothing you could have done—a boy against so many men."

"She shouldn't have died like that. Taken her life with her own hand."

She held him closer. "Your mother only did what you have been willing to do for me, my heart."

He turned his head, spoke in her ear. "I love you, *mo milidh*. More than life."

"As she did you."

He gripped her, and she let him hold her, took the heat that poured from him, let his sorrow burn. When finally he slumped in her arms, she laid him down to sleep.

Now it was Mhoire who lay awake. Her heart ached for the man sprawled on the cold ground beside her, for the boy who had been so cruelly mistreated, for the warrior who had carried such a burden of guilt. No wonder he insisted on protecting her, as if he could make up for what he hadn't been able to do for his mother on that long-ago day. But his love went beyond guardianship, Mhoire realized now. Drosten wanted her to be happy, to be well, to have what she most wanted. And he was willing to give her up—even give up his own future—so that she could have those things.

He lay on his stomach, his face toward her. His hair had dried wispy and golden around his ears, and his lashes lay like strands of flax against his cheeks. The crease between his brows was still there, even in sleep, as if trouble was haunting him still.

Burning from the heat of emotion, Drosten had pushed the blanket down to his waist, exposing his broad back. His skin gleamed golden in the firelight. Mhoire ran her hand along the smooth muscle. He sighed, still sleeping, and the lines in his face relaxed. Gently she kneaded his shoulders. Lowering her head to the crook of his neck, she breathed in his scent. She buried her nose into his skin, rubbed her cheek against his hair. Her hands moved carefully, lovingly, down his arms. Along his knuckles and rough fingers, across his back. Smoothing the knots of guilt, and pushing out the poison of shame.

He rolled onto his side, facing her. His eyes gleamed like the embers of the fire.

He murmured something in his Pictish tongue.

"I've awakened you," she whispered.

He stretched out an arm and brought her to him.

He kissed her so hard she almost stopped breathing. But then she forgot about breathing, only thought about Drosten, and his kisses that warmed her like the sun.

She wanted him. Wanted him close to her. Wanted him to feel her love. Love that was compassion and passion both. Love beyond thought, beyond fear, beyond hope.

She pulled him closer. Unlocked the doors and windows of her soul and flung them wide. And when he whispered her name, his lips on her ear, she knew she could not give him up.

Chapter Twenty-five

Breakfast was eaten quietly. The men, who knew the value of eating even if they weren't hungry, shoveled porridge into their mouths with grim deliberation. Mhoire followed their example.

She chewed on her anger along with her food. Nothing made sense! Someone was after Drosten—he had convinced her of that. But someone was after her, too. Whomever that person was had sent a message to Drosten to kill her. And Drosten would have, if his loyalty to his clan had been stronger than his love for her.

Could that message have been a ploy to get Drosten out of the fort so he could be attacked while alone? That was exactly what had happened. But there was no need for such a maneuver. He routinely left Dun Darach to go hunting. There were all manner of opportunities to hurl an arrow in his back.

Why then send a message to him to kill her? Someone truly must want her dead. That could certainly be Gormach mac Nechtan, who everyone knew hated the Scots and would do anything to ensure the supremacy of the Pictish nation.

But would Gormach attack his only son? What goal would that achieve?

Possession of Dun Darach. It all came back to that. To the broken-down fort that looked to the sea. The gateway to the land they all wanted—the Picts, the Scots, the Britons, the Danes.

And her. Right or wrong, her heart was bound to this land. She had made Dun Darach her home. She had planted its fields, fought for it, almost died for it. And its people had become her clan.

But to whom did Dun Darach really belong?

As her mother's bastard daughter, she had no claim to Dun Darach under Irish law. When her uncle Malcolm was killed by the Danes, Dun Darach became the property of his sister's husband: Colman. Colman had bestowed it upon Mhoire as a dowry. But if Colman didn't know that Mhoire was not his daughter when he arranged the marriage, once he found out, he could take Dun Darach back. Unless, that is, Colman so wanted the alliance with the Picts that he cared naught for her paternity. But for her and Drosten to remain married would put both their lives at risk. Even if Colman wanted them married, someone else wanted them dead.

It was enough to make a woman furious.

She felt Drosten's eyes upon her.

"I'm going back to Dun Darach," she announced.

Relief flooded his face.

"And you're going with me," she added.

His eyes darkened and he opened his mouth to speak, but she cut him off. "I must find out who is behind this. I want to know who thinks he has a better claim to Dun Darach than I do."

"*Mo milidh*—" Drosten looked exasperated. "—you said yourself that you came to Dun Darach under false pretenses. If the fort is not yours, then it certainly can't be mine. I cannot go back with you and pretend I have a legitimate right to it. But if I sever the marriage, I believe I can keep my father away from you. He's a fierce man but he's honorable. He won't kill you out of vengeance and he won't try to take Dun Darach by force."

"Do you want to sever the marriage?"

His voice lowered. "Nay—"

"Are you afraid to fight?"

His brows shot up and he sat back.

"I didn't think so."

"Mhoire, I have a force of only twenty men—"

"And eight women."

He blew out a breath.

"One of whom," she added, "is an excellent archer."

He closed his eyes.

"You are a warrior and a prince. You must have a strategy for this kind of situation. You've been outnumbered before."

Drosten opened his eyes and looked over at Alfred. Alfred raised an eyebrow.

"Thirty against a thousand," Drosten muttered, shaking his head.

"We don't know it's a thousand," Mhoire insisted. "It could be twenty. It could be one. We don't know who is behind this. That is what we must find out."

Drosten ran his hand through his hair.

"If I must give you up," she went on, "if I must give up Dun Darach, I won't do it without a fight." Her hand crept to the small pouch at her breast with its three round pebbles. "My mother wanted me here. Dun Darach was her home. I told myself that because it was my mother's land, it *should* be mine. Why, if I were a Pictish woman . . ."

Mhoire's mouth shut abruptly. But her mind finished her thought. *If I were a Pictish woman, I would have inherited Dun Darach from my mother. It* would *be mine.* And suddenly she knew who it was who wanted them dead.

Drosten stationed Mhoire inside Dun Darach's outer wall. It was not where he wished her to be—he would rather have had her miles away, hidden in some cave, safe. But he knew it would waste his breath to argue with her.

She had insisted they return to Dun Darach. "Our mere presence will provoke an attack," she said. And that had become the plan.

At least inside the wall—in a tiny chamber with a narrow

arrow slit designed for archers—Mhoire would be relatively safe. Besides, she was better with bow and arrow than anyone else, and Drosten needed all the warriors he could muster.

He strode across the courtyard surveying his men, who were checking their weapons and saddling their mounts. Drosten wasn't convinced that Mhoire's strategy was the best course of action, but it delayed separating from her. And if there was a chance that he could stay with her forever—with her brave heart and generous body—he had to seize it.

And he had a plan himself; two plans. Drosten couldn't help but smile remembering Mhoire's challenge. *Surely, he'd been outnumbered before, hadn't he?* Aye, and so plan number one, if it was obvious that the enemy could mow them down, was to surrender and hand over the fort. He would beg for Mhoire's life and the lives of the women. As for himself and his men, well, they all knew that in this case surrender would mean death.

Plan number two was far more complex.

Drosten climbed a ladder to the top of the wall and looked out across the fields. He and Mhoire had crossed those fields openly so that anyone watching from the woods would see them approach and know that they were alive. That would give their enemy two choices. He could attack the fort directly. Or he could harass them so that they wouldn't be able to set foot outside the fort. Then he'd wait until they starved to death.

Drosten's instincts told him this enemy did not like to wait.

He expected an attack to come soon. Thus he had split up his forces. Under the cover of night, more than half of the men had clambered down around the south side of the fort to hide among the rocks between the cliffs and the beach. When the time came, the remaining men would ride north and confront the enemy. After the opposing sides clashed, his men would feign fear and retreat back toward the fort and the open beach. There the bulk of Drosten's warriors would be ready. They'd pin the enemy between the cliffs and the sea and, he hoped, pick them off or drive them into the surf. From her spot in the wall, Mhoire could protect the fort if any of the assailants turned toward it. The other women would be ready, too, with their daggers, their prayers, and pots of boiling water that could be tipped over the wall.

Mhoire had given the women leave to escape during the night—to hide in the caves or seek refuge in the ruined chapel. But they all had refused. Their only concession, after much debate, was to conceal little Oran and a cache of food in the cave they had once shared.

Drosten scanned the countryside, his eyes narrowed. The tide was low, and a wide, hard strip of sand lay exposed below the cobbles. Satisfied with what he saw, he backed down the ladder and threw off his tunic. From his saddle-bag, he drew out a tin of blue paint and lay a broad strip down each arm and both legs, and across his brow. This was how the Picts had fought from the beginning of time: marked by the clan symbols tattooed on their skin and the blue paint that gave them power.

Drosten mounted his horse and signaled to his men to do likewise. He checked for his sword and his axe, made sure they were positioned as he wanted them, and then picked up his round metal shield. Glittering among the square wooden ones his men carried, it identified him as royalty. That was as it should be. He was the enemy's prey. He was the one his assailants would chase to the beach. As the oaken gate swung open, he prayed silently and briefly that he could outrun them.

Mhoire watched them leave. As soon as Drosten had cantered through the gate, she had slipped from her spot in the wall and dashed up a ladder at the north end of the fort so she could keep her eye on what was happening. The sight of Drosten painted a ghostly blue nearly froze her blood.

With scarcely half a dozen men behind him, he galloped

straight across the fields toward the shadowy woods. They could have been a hunting party, heading off under a glorious late-spring sky. Except, that is, for the sense of purpose in their postures, the silent efficiency of their movements.

The small band was only halfway to the woods when dark forms peeled off from the line of trees, as if the trees themselves were splitting in two.

"Oh, God!" Mhoire whispered. They were right there. Men with axes raised, hurling themselves toward Drosten. Fumbling, she shrugged her bow off her shoulder, pulled an arrow from her quiver, notched it, and raised her weapon.

Her eyes once again found Drosten, riveted themselves on his fair head and his white stallion. Saw him lift an arm, strike a blow. "*Run*, my heart, *run! Run to the beach!*" she cried, her words snatched away by the wind.

As if he had heard her, Drosten swirled his horse around and retreated a few yards. Then he stopped and turned to fight again.

How many enemy soldiers were there? Mhoire tried to count. Not hundreds. Tens. She searched the field for the opponent she was expecting to see. Not there. She searched again. Scrutinized every face. *Where was he?*

Then the pack of men swerved as if they were all one body. *Mother of God!* They were coming toward the fort, galloping. "Bring up the water!" she cried to the women below.

Mhoire raised her bow higher and fixed her aim on the man galloping directly behind Drosten. "To the beach!" she muttered through clenched teeth. "Go to the beach, Drosten! Follow your plan!"

Drosten leaned forward onto his stallion's neck and flattened himself so that horse and rider were one clean line. Inch by inch, he pulled away from his pursuer. The attackers still followed, chasing their rabbit. *Why was Drosten leading them to the fort? That wasn't the plan!* Mhoire looked over her shoulder, saw Brigit and Elanta struggling up the ladder with an iron pot, and then turned back to the field. She raised her bow again and, squinting, tracked the rider behind Drosten.

Suddenly, Drosten veered. Sharp to the west. Away from the fort. At the last moment, when his pursuers didn't have a second to consider why, he plunged his horse onto the cobblestone beach. From there, horse and rider skittered down to the sand.

Mhoire raced down the ladder. She whirled and ran for her spot in the wall.

Down in the cave, Oran sat with her knees to her chin. She hated being in the cave. It was cold and dark and wet. Her thin little body, clad only in a threadbare woolen gown, trembled from fright and chill. Every time an icy droplet fell from the ceiling and hit her on the head, she jumped.

Don't make a sound, her mother had said. *Don't move.*

Oran whimpered quietly.

If only she could sit a little closer to the light at the front of the cave, she wouldn't be so afraid. She had never liked the cave, even last winter when her mother and grandmother and the other women had been sleeping in it with her. She had always been afraid of the dark.

The ground was drier near the opening where the sun shone in. If she could just sit there. Then she wouldn't get so dirty and she wouldn't be so afraid. And if a dragon came roaring out of the blackness, she could run outside and get away.

She inched forward. Bit by bit she crept, trying not to make a sound, just like her mother had commanded.

Finally, she reached the patch of sunshine that was warm and bright. But then Oran stilled. She heard noises. Bad noises. Men grunting. Crying out. Horses squealing. Louder. Closer. The terrible clang of iron. Louder still. Coming toward her.

She knew those sounds. She had heard them before. On that awful day. The day that her father lay covered with blood, cut open like a slaughtered pig. And her uncles, and her grandfather, and all the men that she knew. The day her mother cried and could not stop.

Oran rose to her feet and stood in the sunlight, stiff as a stick, her eyes round and her mouth open. Then she ran.

Disbelieving her eyes, Mhoire saw Oran stumble over a boulder, fall, push herself up with her little hands, run a step, and fall again. From where she stood inside the wall, she had a clear view of the child below. And the men fighting just around the curve of the beach.

Mhoire yelled out the arrow slit. "Oran! Go back! Go back!"

But the child was too far away to hear.

Could she protect Oran from above? Not if she hoped to protect the fort as well.

But she couldn't leave Oran alone out there. *Where was Drosten?* She searched for him. *There!* At the far end of the beach. Sweet God, he'd never see the child from that distance.

Mhoire scrutinized the beach again. None of the warriors had yet noticed Oran, who was crawling low to the ground and away from the mayhem. If she could just . . .

She slung her bow over her arm and scrambled out from the wall.

Swiftly, Mhoire padded across the courtyard. All the women were up on the ladders watching the fighting. Good. She dared not tell them about Oran for fear chaos would erupt. With a big pull on the gate, she cracked it open and slipped out.

She made her way around the far side of the fort, letting the fort itself shield her from the battle. It was a steep, rough descent to the beach. She used the cracks in the rock for toeholds and handholds, bruising her fingers and scraping her shins. Near the bottom, the rocks were slimy with seaweed, and she slipped and slid until her palms were scraped raw.

Mhoire's feet hit the soft sand. Before her was a huge

boulder. Oran was on the other side of it. She could hear her whimpering and choking on her sobs.

And another voice. A man's voice. One she knew.

She plunged forward toward the sounds.

Irwin. Holding Oran by the arm. He must have heard the din of the battle. He must have come to help.

"Thank God you are here," Mhoire panted. "We must get her up to the fort."

She reached for Oran, but Irwin's grasp tightened, and he yanked her closer to his side. Oran let out a low wail.

Mhoire stopped.

"You thought I was a good neighbor?" Irwin's mouth twisted like a snake, and his pale brows shot up.

Him? Irwin was their enemy? Why?

"Give her to me!" Mhoire hissed. "God damn you to hell! Give her to me."

"Drop the bow first."

Oh, no. That would leave her defenseless. She had given her dagger to Nila. Her bow was her only weapon.

She stalled. "These are your men fighting here?"

"Nay. These are Britons."

"*Britons?* I don't understand."

"They're my friends."

Mhoire's eyes widened. "You are friends with the Britons? Why? You don't need them. You have everything!"

"Except power." Clutching a terrified Oran with one hand, Irwin drew his sword from its scabbard with the other. He pressed the point into the sand and leaned on it. "You thought I wanted *you,* didn't you?" He cocked an eyebrow. "I would have taken you, if I could have gotten rid of Drosten mac Nechtan. I had hoped the wild boar would tear him apart for me. For a time, I thought you might manage to chase him back to his own country—you were so determined. But then you married the man. When I couldn't have you at all, I realized I really didn't need you. And I certainly didn't want him around."

"But why are you fighting for Dun Darach now? You

could have taken it easily when only the women were here."

"You know I could not have seized it when it was in the hands of the Scots, with no justification. That would be stealing from a neighbor, and the king of Dal Riata would have had me hung. But now everything has fallen into place. We lured Drosten mac Nechtan, the great Pictish warrior, here. You married him, which transferred Dun Darach to the Picts. Now, with the help of our new allies, the Britons, we can kill Drosten and take over Dun Darach at the same time."

"Why do you say 'we'?"

Irwin opened his mouth to answer and then clamped it shut. His eyes focused on something behind Mhoire.

She turned, and her heart clenched in her chest.

Chapter Twenty-six

"It is you after all," Mhoire whispered.

Colman stood a few paces away at the base of the cliff, a gleam of triumph in his eyes. He took a step toward her. "Drop the bow."

She let the weapon fall. Hatred, like nausea, roiled within her.

"I never knew you to be sharp-witted," Colman said.

"You never knew me at all."

"I knew you as well as I wanted to." He took a few more steps toward her. "You made a lucky guess."

"Nay. I realized that a Pict would never want to kill me. The Picts need me to stay alive. They need me to have children with their prince. Under Pictish law, the only way they can keep Dun Darach is through my daughters. Gormach mac Nectan would never have ordered Drosten to kill me."

"Ah, you show a bit of wit, my child."

"I am not your child."

"Nay. You are *her* child."

"And I'm proud to be! She was a worthy woman!"

"You have no idea what your mother was."

"I know what you are. A drunkard and a bully and a liar."

A ruddy flush mottled Colman's face.

Mhoire let her rage flame. "You lured the Picts into this. You had no intention of honoring Drosten's presence on

191

this land. You had no desire for an alliance with his people."

"Why should I?" Colman spit out. "The Picts have fought against us for centuries. They slaughtered our ancestors. Now we have a chance to wipe them out."

"With the Danes hard upon them, and the Britons at their back. And now you, an Irishman, are joining hands with their enemies." Mhoire shook her head in disgust. "And your first goal is to murder their best commander. With the help of this . . . rat here." She gestured to Irwin and then fixed her eyes on Colman. "What do you get from this? What do you get for killing Drosten?"

"Fame." Colman's eyes glittered green.

"And you would kill me for that as well?"

"Who are you to me?"

"I shared your house! I mended your clothes, made your candles, helped prepare your food, healed your servants!"

"You are her child, not mine."

Mhoire drew herself up. "I'm proud of that."

"You shouldn't be." The muscles in Colman's neck tightened. "I saved her, you know. She was pregnant before we even married. If your grandfather had known, he would have cast her out. Sent her to the convent and locked her away. But I took her. I married her."

"She never loved you."

"She might have!" Colman roared.

"Nay. Never. Not the way you treated her."

"You insolent girl! Don't speak to me like that!"

Mhoire stared at him, tried to gather her wits. Colman had a dagger at his hip. Irwin held Oran in one hand and his sword in another. Her bow was lying in the sand. Where was Drosten? *Drosten!*

"So this is your revenge, is it?" Mhoire made a sweeping gesture with her arm and as she did so, took a step toward the boulders. "You take my mother's land, the land she loved, and use it to further your own ambition."

Colman shrugged.

"Does the king of Dal Riata know?" Mhoire asked, stepping back again.

"Of course, the king knows."

"But he's not part of this, is he? I see how few men you have here." She gestured again, took another backward step. "If the king supported you, there would be a battalion of warriors on this beach, not a few dozen. Is he humoring you? Is he amused by this?"

Another wave of color saturated Colman's face. "The king knows the value of destroying the Picts."

"You fools! What value? The value of avenging an ancient wrong? What good is that when the Danes are at our doorstep? How will that help when they burn our forts and kill our men and take our children as slaves? You need the Picts as friends, not enemies!"

Colman gave her a cold stare. "We need Drosten mac Gormach dead."

"And you have been using me to achieve that," she stated flatly.

"I needed to get him away from his homeland, away from the bulk of his forces. I needed to get him someplace where he would be vulnerable."

"But you haven't been able to get rid of him, have you? He'll survive this battle today."

"Nay. Today, I will kill him."

"How can you be so certain?"

A malevolent smile split Colman's face. "He'll give himself up. Once he sees that I have you."

Mhoire's eyes narrowed into slits. "You don't have me. You will never have me. Just as you never truly had my mother."

Colman's smile disappeared, and he lunged for her.

Oran shrieked. Mhoire stumbled back and scrambled behind a boulder. Reaching behind her neck, she pulled an arrow from her quiver and clenched it in her fist like a dagger. Suddenly, Colman whipped in front of her. She plunged the arrow into his chest.

It hit his leather breastplate and bounced off.

Colman staggered, cursed, and reached for her arm. She kicked him hard in the shins. He recoiled. She stabbed again. Higher. Aimed for his neck. But Colman saw her thrust coming and jerked back.

There was movement at her side. *Irwin!* Diving toward her with his sword.

Oran screamed—a shrill animal sound—and hurled herself at Irwin's knees.

Mhoire swung around to Colman, sweat pouring in her eyes, her arrow raised high like a spear.

Colman's jaw clenched and his brows lowered. She knew he was ready for her this time.

Her grasp tightened on her arrow.

She swung her arm. But before it completed its arc, a blood-curdling yell cut the air.

Colman's mouth opened in horror, and he sank to his knees. Blood snaked around his neck and oozed down his chest and his arms and his hands. He lowered his eyes to his limbs and then raised them to meet hers. He stared at her, wide-eyed. And then his pupils clouded, and he fell face down in the sand.

Towering over him stood Gormach mac Nechtan, his long gray hair as wild as the wind and his scar a lightning gash down his face.

Mhoire went rigid, and the sound of her own pulse roared in her ears. Then she felt a hand cover her fist, which still clutched the arrow. Gently, it pried apart her fingers. A quiet voice spoke in her ear. "Let me have the arrow, *mo milidh*. It's over now."

Chapter Twenty-seven

There was no celebration in the hall.

Gormach's warriors, who had crashed onto the beach like a tidal wave, had added their force to Drosten's handful of men and quickly ended the battle. But the victory over Colman and Irwin did not ensure their peace.

"Don't you think that the Dal Riata king will leave us be?" Mhoire asked, reaching for Drosten's hand. They were sharing a bench in front of the hearth fire. Gormach sat on a second bench that was positioned across from them. Elanta was busying herself nearby with a pot of nettle soup, and Nila was making an infusion of chamomile to settle Mhoire's nerves.

Drosten squeezed her hand. "He didn't contribute much to this skirmish, that is true. But I doubt that he will ignore us altogether."

Mhoire looked over at Drosten's father. Strain had tightened his face, leaving long grooves down the sides of his mouth. "This is not how you wanted it to be, is it?"

"Nay, lass. I wanted to avoid war with the Scots and the Irish. That's why I arranged your marriage to my son. It would not be wise to try to keep Dun Darach through force. If the Dal Riata king decided to lay siege, we would have to bring in an army from Pictland. Then we'd have an all-out war. We can't fight the Danes, the Britons, and the Scots at the same time."

"What are you saying?" Mhoire asked.

Drosten slipped his arm across her shoulders. "He's saying that we can't stay here."

"But we must!" She turned to him. "Everyone here needs us. We can't abandon these women again. Besides, this is my home."

Gormach answered. "I traveled here to congratulate you on your marriage," he said roughly. "I didn't know what trouble you were in. So I take no joy in making you leave. But I cannot allow my son to fight a worthless war. Either the both of you come to Pictland, or you divorce."

Drosten's arm tightened across her shoulders and drew her closer to his side. "My father is right, Mhoire. We must go back. If we had even a small claim to Dun Darach, we might manage to stay. We could possibly even negotiate an agreement with your king. But as it is, a Pictish presence here could only be seen as an act of aggression—thievery—and your king's pride would force him to confront us on the battlefield."

"But surely there's got to be another choice!" Mhoire cried. She appealed to Nila and Elanta, her eyes wild. "Isn't there among you some connection to my grandfather? Some thread of relation? Could any of you inherit the fort? Could Drosten and I stay by your favor?"

Elanta looked at Nila. Calmly, Nila poured the chamomile infusion into a cup, wiped her hands on her skirt, and extended the cup to Mhoire.

"Drink this down, child," she said firmly. "Then we'll walk to the chapel."

Nila took the lead. Mhoire, Drosten, and Gormach followed, along with most of the other women and some of Drosten's soldiers. They tramped across the rough fields and through the dark woods, and finally arrived at the grounds of the ruined chapel.

Silently, they passed through the grove of cherry trees that encircled the sacred building. When they reached the low hillside that protected the chapel on three sides, Nila headed up. The others followed.

They found themselves inside a grove of small, gnarled trees. "These are oak trees," Mhoire whispered, with wonder in her voice. "*Dun Darach*—'Fort of the Oaks.' "

Their trunks grew thick and solid. Their limbs, twisted by the wind and their own natural yearnings, reached out like sinewed arms. And in the center of the grove, in a patch of bright green moss, stood a monolithic stone, twice the height of a man and covered with intricate designs. Nila stopped beside it.

Tentatively, Mhoire approached the stone, and ran her hand over the carvings. She recognized a falcon and a lightning rod. Below them was an image of a sword and, next to it, a boat. Sitting in the boat was a woman with her arms crossed over her breasts.

"What does this mean?" Gormach asked. "This is a Pictish stone."

Nila watched Mhoire. "Shall I tell you about your real father?"

Mhoire nodded, her hand still tracing the designs.

"He was badly wounded in a battle with the Britons that took place a few miles from here. He needed care, but he was far from home and only a few of the soldiers he commanded were alive. Fearing he would not survive a journey back to Pictland, his men brought him here to the chapel, and asked for sanctuary. The monks called upon your mother to help tend him because she was skilled with herbs."

Mhoire turned to Nila and stared. "You are saying my father is a Pict?"

Nila touched Mhoire's arm. "*Was* a Pict, my child. He died."

"Those are our clan symbols," Gormach said. He pointed to the falcon and the lightning rod. "But what do the other carvings mean?"

"Mhoire's mother and the Pictish leader fell in love," Nila went on. "They intended to slip away, to go back together to Pictland, as soon as he was well enough to travel. One of the monks married them."

Mhoire gasped. Her eyes flew to Drosten. He cocked a brow. "And what happened?" she asked.

"Your grandfather didn't know that the young man your mother was tending at the monastery was a Pict. And, of course, their marriage was a secret. But she became pregnant. And, contrary to what Colman believes, your grandfather found out about it. He sent his men to the monastery and they killed your father in cold blood."

Nila paused. The leaves of the oak trees whispered.

"Shortly after, Colman came through with his band of men. They had sailed from Ireland to help in the war against the Picts. Your grandfather gave Colman shelter, and the day after Colman saw your mother, he asked for her hand. To her credit, your mother told him the truth, that she was carrying another man's child. But Colman married her anyway. I believe he thought the pregnancy wouldn't matter. He didn't realize the strength of your mother's love for her Pictish warrior."

"She was miserable with Colman."

"Aye. But what choice did she have? No man here would marry her. And she did not want her child to grow up in shame."

"Did Colman murder my mother? One day she was fine, and the next . . ."

"I don't know, my child," Nila answered quietly. "It's possible."

Mhoire looked at Drosten and bit her lip. "We are not brother and sister, I hope."

Gormach peered at Nila. "What was the Pictish man's name?"

"Aed mac Domnall."

Gormach shook his head. "No close relation."

"And so Dun Darach is ours," Drosten said, his eyes gleaming. He walked up to the stone. "The Pictish leader—" He traced the falcon with his fingertips. "—marries the Scottish princess." He touched the figure of the woman in the boat. "Who is sent across the sea to Ireland."

He turned to face Mhoire and rested his hands lightly on

her shoulders. "They have a daughter, who under Pictish law inherits her mother's property." He lifted a hand and rubbed a rough thumb along Mhoire's cheekbone. Then he looked over her shoulder at Nila. "Is there proof of this marriage, old woman?"

"Aye," she answered with a chuckle, the first bit of laughter Mhoire had heard from her lips. "It's in the monastery's record book. And we hid that in the cellar so the Danes wouldn't burn it."

"Well, then," Drosten said, with a slow smile. "There's no denying this."

"And all of you women knew this secret but me?" Mhoire moaned. She turned under Drosten's hold and scanned the faces of the others. The women looked sheepish. Drosten's soldiers seemed to be in shock.

Drosten's hands tightened on Mhoire's shoulders. "Who carved the stone?" he asked.

"My husband," Nila answered, chuckling again. "He was one of Aed's men. Instead of returning to Pictland, he stayed here and we farmed."

Mhoire gaped at Nila. "You married a Pict? That means that Elanta . . . and Oran . . ."

"Are somewhat Pictish. Aye."

"No wonder you didn't object to having rough Pictish men around the fort."

Drosten bent close to her face, his eyes dark and serious. "And you, *mo milidh*? Do you object?"

Mhoire smiled up at him. "Nay." She drew his lips down to hers. "I believe I'm turning a bit rough myself."

Epilogue

The age of the Picts ended before the close of the ninth century. What happened to this powerful society? Did the Scots overcome the Picts through treachery or force during a vulnerable time when they were under attack by Vikings? Or did intermarriage and succession lead to a transfer of power? With no written historical record to guide us, we can only guess.

What historians do know is that the Picts suffered a century of genocide by the Vikings. History also tells us that by 845, Kenneth mac Alpin, a Scot with a supposedly Pictish mother, was ruler of both Dal Riata and Pictland. He became the founder of a new dynasty, one that was neither Irish nor Pictish but was henceforth known as Scotland.

And the Picts entered the realm of mythology. Their language disappeared, along with their rulers. They might have become a forgotten people, except for the images they left behind, engraved on magnificent standing stones that still grace the glens of their homeland.